EIGHTEEN AGAINST ONE!

"Get him, damn it! Kill him!" Parley's men came toward him in a wild charge.

He staggered to his feet and lunged through the trees. Crispin was hurt, how badly he did not know, but his mind was filled with panic. He had to get away.

Suddenly he saw the ravine narrow before him. He ran at the opening and he was on the lip of a cliff, a dry waterfall!

He tried to slow down, to stop himself, but his impetus was too great. He felt himself go over, his fingers clawed at the rocks.

The last thing he knew was a faint circle of light above and then darkness closed in . . .

THE MAN FROM SKIBBEREEN

LOUIS L'AMOUR

BANTAM BOOKS · TORONTO · NEW YORK · LONDON

THE MAN FROM SKIBBEREEN

A Bantam Book | July 1973

2nd printing .... *July 1973*	*8th printing* .... *April 1976*	
3rd printing .. *September 1973*	*9th printing* .. *February 1977*	
4th printing ...... *October 1973*	*10th printing* .... *July 1977*	
5th printing .... *July 1974*	*11th printing* .... *May 1978*	
6th printing .... *August 1975*	*12th printing* .. *February 1979*	
7th printing ...... *October 1975*	*13th printing* .... *October 1979*	

14th printing .... *January 1980*

15th printing

ISBN 0-553-13879-0

Published simultaneously in the United States and Canada

Bantam Books are published by Bantam Books, Inc. Its trade-
mark, consisting of the words "Bantam Books" and the por-
trayal of a bantam, is Registered in U.S. Patent and Trademark
Office and in other countries. Marca Registrada. Bantam
Books, Inc., 666 Fifth Avenue, New York, New York 10019.

PRINTED IN THE UNITED STATES OF AMERICA

Chapter One

Crispin Mayo had a wish to walk the high land with the company of eagles and the shadow of clouds, so he strode away to Bantry Bay and shipped aboard a windjammer as an able-bodied seaman. It was his first voyage on such a vessel, although he had fished upon deep water since childhood, and knew a marlinspike from a hickory fid before he was six.

He jumped his ship in Boston Town and hied himself off along the dark streets, trusting no man and steering a course sheer of grog shops and the painted girls who lay traps for trusting sailormen.

When the dawning came upon him he was beyond the city's streets and walking along country lanes with stone walls to left and right like there'd been at home in County Cork. He stayed shy of main-travelled roads for fear that if they found him they'd ship him home again, and he'd yet to see a mountain. So he begged a meal here, chopped wood for one there, and slept by the night in a haystack or a farmer's barn. And after sleeping in the barn, if he had an egg or two of the farmer's chickens, who is to blame him for that? After all, a large-shouldered Irish lad comes easy upon hunger.

He had no blackthorn stick, so he cut one of oak from a fallen branch with a fine heft to it that lay handy to the road. If only one man came for him, or even two, he'd be after tearin' down their meathouse with his fists, but if they came against him in numbers the stick might be handy. Crossing a pasture once a bull came upon him, a bull with no taste for the singing of Ballinascarty songs, but he laid the bull flat with a blow between the horns and went his way a-singing.

Somebody said while he listened that in a westward land they were building a railroad, and paying strong lads for the driving of steel, so he went that way and a hiring-man put him on a train. He sat royally upon the cushions then, and west he went with Paddy Gallagher, Tommy O'Brien and Mick Shannon riding beside him, bound for the end of track, wherever that might be, and nobody caring the least.

The houses thinned out and the villages disappeared and when they had ridden the night through and day was come they were crossing a vast plain of grass, with the blue sky above and the train chugging down a fresh-laid track into a newborn land.

All day they rode, and through the night and the day again, seeing only the grass, the sky, and far in the distance some woolly black cows, until a time came when the train clanked and squealed to a stop. The man in the blue suit and cap got down and walked slowly forward along the track toward a small building painted a dull red.

It was very hot, very still, and the black flies buzzed about. Cris Mayo stepped down to stretch his legs and saw shade, so he walked yonder and sat beneath a cottonwood; and there the leaves brushed together, whispering stories to the wind, and Cris Mayo closed his eyes, liking the smell of the sun upon the grass and the sound of a trickle of water from somewhere close. He would get a drink before he boarded the train again, but first he would sit quiet for a moment. Far off he could hear voices calling in the shack, he heard the conductor swear, and sometime along there he closed his eyes, just for a bit.

He opened them suddenly to a shrill whistle blowing, heard the grind of the train starting and came swiftly to his feet, sprinting for the track. He went up the slight bank, his feet slipped on the gravel, and he fell. The train was gathering speed. Swearing, he ran, but a fast forty rods only left him panting and the train disappearing, slowly drawing into itself with distance and the narrowing track.

He stood staring and alone. Only the twin rails before

2

and behind him, and the sky and grass large all about. He trudged down the track, walking back to the small station, a box of a place with a signal pole before it and a sidetrack alongside the main line.

He wondered why they laid the ties so that a man could not walk upon them decently, but had to go a step and a half and then a step or so . . . arrah, a bothersome thing!

It was hot, and there was nothing about but a bird, a meadow lark somebody had said; but with a fine sound to it, not like any lark he had heard, yet lovely still.

The station was there, two windows facing him with blank eyes and a closed door—why, in God's name, on such a hot day? He called out, but no one answered, his voice falling empty away from the dull red wall.

Under his hand the door opened, and he spoke inquiringly into the room. A telegraph key chattered, chattered like the teeth of a frightened banshee. He walked in, leaving the door standing, but nobody was there, the room was empty. It looked empty, it felt empty, it was empty. The second room, for sleeping, also empty.

The bed was unmade. How his old grandmother would have gone on about that, the middle of the day and the bed not made! A shocking thing, not to be believed.

There was the station room with a bench for sitting, there was the bedroom with the unmade bed and a homemade washstand, and some old clothes on pegs. He stepped through the back door and stopped of a sudden, for there was the darkness of a stain on the stoop there, a stain of blood.

Blood looks much the same when spilled in Skibbereen or in Boston or on the western plains, and Cris Mayo had seen a bit of blood in his time. Something or somebody had bled here, bled a sight more than was good for him. Yet when his eyes looked beyond there was nothing but the wide waving grass and the sky over it, with them meeting yonder, far off.

All that empty land, he thought, and not a potato planted. A dreadful waste of soil. He went back within:

3

a snug place for all it was only a shack, and built well against the winter to come. The instrument clicked angrily but he knew nothing of its operation. There was a chair beside it, and papers strewn all about the tiny desk with a pencil laid down as if the owner had just stepped away.

Was there anybody here at all, then? Or had they found him injured and taken him aboard the train? What had happened to the man? Had he hurt himself, or been attacked? This was not Ireland, and Cris was a far piece from Clonakilty. There might be things here, deadly things, of which he did not know.

The key was chattering, so he went to it and put his finger on it and chattered right back at them, a wild burst and then another.

Silence—utter, astonished silence.

Then the machine erupted into a wild crescendo of sound, a quick, excited racket. When it was silent again, he touched the key just once.

A short volley of clicks, then silence. He touched the key again.

At least they knew that someone was here. When he was discovered missing from the train, they would surely know it was he who was at the station; yet would they come in time?

For the first time he thought of eating and drinking. There must be something here, for the station agent or whatever he was called had to have supplies. He went into the bedroom and looked for food.

It was there, of course. A couple of sides of bacon, a ham, jerked beef, dried apples, some coffee, flour . . . and there was a stove and a lamp. In the station room there had also been a couple of red lanterns. He wouldn't lack for light.

He was getting up from peering into the lower part of the food box when he saw the rifle. It was on the floor, half under the bed. He picked it up carefully. It was almost new. When he worked the lever, it ejected a spent shell. There was a spot of blood on the floor near where the gun had lain, and what appeared to be blood on the stock.

Building a fire in the stove, he made coffee, fried a dozen pieces of bacon, found some stale biscuits, and ate, sitting by the window with his eyes on the empty grass out there. When he had finished and washed the cup and plate, he tapped the key again. At once it sprang to life, chattering away with a will. It seemed to be asking questions, but he had no idea of how to answer, save with the single click.

The sun was sinking, the sky a glory of color, the grass ablaze with red.

He thought of the patch of blood by the back door and the vanished telegrapher. Snatches of conversation overheard on the train returned to trouble him. There was supposed to have been a signal on the pole near the track, and there had been none.

He went to the door and looked down the track. Nothing. The twin rails merged and vanished. Right in front of the station there was a sidetrack that would take about two dozen cars; a small plank platform; a bench against the station wall. Sitting on the bench was a square box he had not noticed until now. He recalled seeing it in the car near where the brakeman sat. He tested the weight: heavy.

Picking it up, he carried it into the station and put it down on the floor. Using a hammer that lay there with a few other tools, he opened the box.

Ammunition. Bullets for the rifle.

It was growing dark inside, yet he hesitated to light a lamp. What was out there? Was there anything?

Indians?

The boys on the train had talked about them. Likely to scalp a man, they said, big, ugly devils, they said, all painted and screeching. They'd come sneaking through the grass with bows, arrows and tomahawks. Maybe the boys had only been trying to scare him. He wasn't afraid of any bloody red devils, not him. Not Crispin Mayo who had whipped those three lads from Dublin, whipped them all at once, and with bare fists. Thrashed them good, he had. And all because of a girl from Baltimore, that little seaport down the coast from his home in County Cork.

5

He filled his cup again. The sun was gone, the sky was streaked with sullen red. A wind blew over the grass, a wind with the smell of far-off. He wondered what was out there, over the distant rim of the world from which the long wind blew.

If he could work that instrument, he might get them to send a train for him. A train? For one Irish immigrant? Ah, not likely, that.

He took up the rifle again, handling it gingerly. He had never fired a rifle, although he had heard much talk of it, had been told all about it by an uncle who had served in the French Army, and who, when drunk, persisted in going through all the instruction he had been given in the use of firearms. Cris heard it over and over, but whether Uncle Pat knew what he was talking about, he had no idea.

How had Cris Mayo gotten into this fix, anyway? From fighting. Restlessness, fighting, and a blue-eyed girl with freckles on her nose. After he'd walloped the three Dubliners, he'd gone down to Skibbereen and fought the two O'Sullivans. Broad, fine lads they were, and quick with their fists, but not so quick as himself, nor so strong.

He battered them, and all in good fun, too, but when he returned to his job he was discharged.

Oh, he had seen that coming! They wanted to be rid of him from the moment he walked out with Barney Kinsella's daughter, her that another had set his eyes upon. They wished him gone, so when the excuse offered, they sent him packing.

He'd started in to fish the waters off the Old Head of Kinsale, Rosscarbery, and the Bay of Glandore, to fish very seriously indeed; and it was the selling of fish that allowed him to put by a bit to start him on his own way.

A rough enough time he had of it until he found himself aboardship. Then he'd been all right, because he was quick with his hands and a good man at rigging, splicing or handling sail; but most of the boys along the shores of Kerry or Cork could have done as well.

Now he was alone here, in this far land, marooned in a

tiny telegraph shack beside a railroad that went to nowhere. Westward they were laying track across the wide prairie, but the only place before them that he'd heard of was Hell-on-Wheels, the moving town at the end of the tracks. No, there was a fort, too, somewhere out there. He forgot its name.

Black outside now . . . it was black with a storm coming and no stars. Leaves rustled and the grass bent before the wind. A sudden burst of that wind slammed against the walls and lightning flashed, once and again. Peering out the back window, he saw the rain coming in a solid wall, and *something . . . something else was there!*

Lightning flared once more. Something ghastly and white! Something rain-wet and walking, walking straight and stiff toward the shack! The blackness closed in and Cris Mayo stared, his throat gripped with superstitious terror. The lightning flamed, a sharp wicked stroke that struck somewhere near, and in its brightness the white thing lay sprawled on the grass not twenty feet from the shack: clearly, in that instant, a naked man.

Fear forgotten, Cris Mayo slammed open the door and lunged across the stoop into the storm. Wind whipped at him, smashed his breath back down his throat, lashed him with sheets of rain. Head down, he plunged the few yards to the fallen man and his hands grasped the wet, cold body, half-dragging, half-carrying it in through the door. As he dropped it, a flare of lightning showed him what seemed two bulletholes, black and round, in the man's body.

Shoving hard, he forced the door shut against the wind, and stood a moment to catch his breath. Then he struck a light and held it to the lamp's wick. Replacing the chimney, he carried the lamp into the room where the bed was, then returned for the man.

With a dirty towel he wiped him dry, then covered him with the bed's blankets. He filled a kettle and put it on the stove to heat. He found a packet of tea in the cabinet and filled a pot. There was little enough he knew about wounds, but he'd heard it said that tea was good for shock, and certainly it was good for a man as wet and cold as this one. Rummaging around, he found a bottle of whiskey, and put it by.

The man's skull was a mess. He'd been horribly beaten about the head, and shot twice. One of the bullets had gone through. The other must be someplace inside him. Obviously, he had been stripped and left for dead.

Indians? The man's scalp was not taken, and Indians would surely have burned the shack and taken what else they wanted; yet who else would want to rob a poor man such as this? And where were they now? Miles it was, many miles, to any place a man other than an Indian was likely to be. How and why had they come to this empty spot? Such a far place, and then not even to take his rifle or food? It made no sense.

Was this man the missing station agent? And why a station here at all? Of course, there was a spring yonder, and a well near the house, and it might be that they planned a water tank here.

Cris had not really searched the place, but now he did it. The first thing he found was a pistol with an old worn scabbard that had seen use and much care, and belt for ammunition. He thought for a moment, shrugged, then belted on the gun. He had never used such a gun but he could at least fire it *at* somebody.

The man muttered unintelligibly in his delirium, then subsided. After a moment he sat up suddenly. "Help," he said, "help me." He looked at Mayo, but whether he saw him or not was a question.

"I've some tea, man. Drink it down now, I'm thinkin' it will help."

The wounded man managed a couple of swallows. He lay down again, muttered, and slept.

Cris made sure the man was covered, then blew out the light and with rifle and pistol at hand, sat down in a chair against the wall by the bedroom window and tried to relax. Thunder rolled, lightning flashed, and the rain beat against roof and wall and window, but Cris began to nod and closed his eyes.

Through pounding rain a rider came from the night, lightning picking highlights from his glistening slicker, throwing deeper shadow under the turned-down hat-brim.

The rider sat his restive mount, peering through the darkness at the station, then suddenly swung his horse and rode away. Crispin Mayo did not look out. He did not see the vanishing rider.

Crispin Mayo was asleep.

Chapter Two

Cris Mayo opened his eyes to the gray of dawn, the silver rails before his eyes, the rain-wet grass stretching away forever. At first he sat still, looking through the window, remembering where he was, hearing the breathing of the man on the bed.

Cris could recall no day when he had not risen before the first light. There had always been a furrow to plow, fish to catch, hay to stack, turf to cut. He liked the turf-cutting best, for all the hard work it was. The poor layers on top must be laid aside to get at the black, brittle stuff that burned well, and that was always deep down.

He got to his feet, stretching his stiff muscles and scratching his head. He glanced at the wounded man. His face was haggard, and his breathing ragged . . . if you could call it breathing.

Cris went to the stove, found some glowing coals among the gray wood ash and fed in some bark shredded between his palms, then some slivers of pine. He added fuel as the flames climbed, replaced the lid and went to the water barrel. The spigot yielded only a few drops.

Taking the wooden bucket, he went to the well and drew water. There was a tin dipper, and he tasted the water. It was good, a little brackish, but good. It needed a dozen trips to fill the barrel, and then he filled the bucket, for a man never knew when water would be needed and he had no wish to be without it. Anyway, it was the pattern of his life. If a bucket was empty, you filled it. If a woodbox was empty, you filled that, too.

There were pink streaks in the sky. He looked slowly

around. He had heard the trickle of water when he'd rested under the cottonwoods, so after a glance around, he walked to them. It was quiet there, among the trees, and there was a good bit of fuel and kindling to be gathered from the ground where limbs had fallen after windstorms.

He found the stream, a tiny one, and followed it a quarter of a mile to a notch in the hills where it flowed from a crack under a slab of rock.

Again he looked around, but there was nothing in sight or hearing, not even a bird.

The wounded man was still sleeping when Cris walked back to the shack, so he fried bacon, made coffee, and ate. When he had finished the bacon he dipped stale biscuits in the grease and ate that. The coffee tasted good.

Cris Mayo was a broad, powerful young man, five feet ten inches tall, weighing nearly one hundred and ninety. He had worked hard all his life and his hands were strong from the lifting and digging. As he drank his coffee he thought about what he must do.

He knew from overheard talk that the end of track was far to the west and the nearest trackside settlement was over a hundred miles from here. Fort Sanders, that was the name! About forty miles west there was a slough from which the trains pumped water, but there was nothing there, nothing at all but the water and the cattails that surrounded it.

He had no idea what he should do, or could do. He had no idea when there would be another train, for the trains carrying track-laying materials and supplies to the end of the line were few. It might be today, tomorrow, or a week from now. And it was a strange land in which he found himself, a land such as he had never seen. It was nothing like the cozy green hills of Ireland; only the endless grass stirring with the wind, and of course there was *that* . . . the wind. It blew forever, softly, gently, but always, it seemed. He walked outside and looked through the dancing heat waves toward the horizon. Only those twin rails that melted together in the distance, and not even a cloud in the sky this morning. The storm had come suddenly, gone suddenly. Well, that at least was like Ireland, the abrupt weather changes.

He went again to the wounded man, who appeared to be worse. He muttered, seemed to argue, to protest, none of it making sense. Cris Mayo listened and tried to think out what must have happened.

Somebody had tried to kill this man . . . why? Not Indians, but somebody else. *Why?* The man could have had nothing of value, and they had not robbed the station. Had the coming of the train prevented that? It could be, but then why had they not come back since? Or was there another reason than robbery? Something he did not know?

Being an Irishman, he thought of politics. An Irishman is born to politics and to contention. There had always been contention with England, and often among their own people. The tribes and the septs had fought time and again. Was this something like that?

Cris Mayo had never thought of himself as a bright man. He knew how to work and how to fight. He had acquired the ordinary skills that a working man knows, the easy ways to lift, the way to tip a barrel or a box, the way to rig a block and tackle for the best results. He knew something of his own country's history, but he knew nothing of America or the politics of it.

There had been a war recently, of course he knew that. A war between the states over whether they should remain one country or divide into two, and slavery had been involved.

He had no use for slavers. Ireland had had enough of that, as had most other countries. The Danes had raided the coasts of Ireland, as had the Algerians, for slavery had been a way of life the world around until men began to build machines to do the work for them. It was the same in Africa itself, he'd heard talk of that. Over there in the tribal wars they enslaved their prisoners or sold them . . . it had been that way forever, so far as he knew; and like as not, all over the world, too.

Now the American war was over, and a good many Irishmen had died in it. He'd had acquaintances who

12

had shipped over the sea to fight for the North, but with the war finished, there was little reason to believe that this muddle here had anything to do with it.

So what then? A robbery? The men working on the railroad must be paid somehow, and the money must be shipped westward to where they were; so that might be it, but why kill the station agent? And strip his carcass?

Wait now! Was the holdup to take place here? He thought of that and the logic of it appealed, yet several things disturbed him. Sitting staring out over the grasslands, he tried to think of how it might be done. That was important, but even more important was the getting away. That was the thing. It was one thing to get the boodle, another to get to where it could be spent. And where did one go from here?

He had never seen a map of the country, and his only knowledge of it was from one of his companions on the train, Mick Shannon, who had been a soldier in the Army three years ago, and had served out here. To the south there was a stretch inhabited by Indians. America had friendly Indians in the eastern part, and wild, savage Indians in the west . . . which was right south of here. Beyond that was Texas, and from what he had heard of Texas, anything might happen there.

To the north there were empty plains, with more Indians ready with their scalping knives. To the west somewhere were mountains.

Where then would they go, if robbery was the idea? And what was more to the point, where were they *now?*

He was sorry he had thought of that, for they must be somewhere near, and that meant a camp, a base of operations, a place to wait until the train came.

When he went to the wounded man again, his eyes were open and he was staring at the ceiling. Cris stood beside the bed and after a minute he said, "I'll fix some broth. You'll be well to get something inside you, man."

The man's eyes turned, and there was fear in them. "I am Cris Mayo," Cris said. "I got left behind when the train stopped. I was headed for the end of track to be a-helpin' with the liftin' of rails and the swingin' of hammers, like."

13

He stirred the fire and shaved some beef jerky into the hot water he'd kept, and after a bit of stirring he carried it to the wounded man and spooned some of it into him. The man took half a dozen spoons and then shook his head weakly.

"You've been beaten," Cris said, "and shot, and stripped."

The man stared at him, his lips fumbling at words that wouldn't come.

"I found you out back." Cris pointed. "You came up through the rain. It is in my mind that you were hauled away from here, hidden and left for dead. It was not Indians, I think?"

"No."

It was the first word. The man closed his eyes.

Cris hesitated. The man should rest, but desperately he needed to know. "Why?" he asked.

The man shook his head. Cris squatted on his heels. "How many?" he said. "You'd best tell me. They might come back."

The eyes opened. "The train!" he whispered hoarsely. "Sherman!"

"How many? Who are they?"

"Ma . . . many. Nine, ten . . . more." The wounded man struggled to rise, got to his elbows. "Call . . . must call! Help me!"

"You lie down now. Take it easy, man. You'll be needing rest. There's time—"

"No! No time! The train!"

"Is it a holdup?"

"Sherman . . . it is Sherman." The man's voice trailed off and he fainted, falling back upon the bed.

Sherman? He knew nothing of outlaws in the west. Whoever this Sherman was, he had the telegrapher scared. Mayo walked from front to back, staring out at the grasslands. They were returning, a lot of them, and they'd try to stop the train . . . but when? When was a train coming and why did they want to stop it?

"Crispin Mayo," he said aloud, "this is no affair of yours. Get out of here, hide down yonder where the trees grow. You have no part in this. You came over

14

from County Cork to lay track, and you'd best be at it, and nothing else at all."

Yet he was not a callous brute, he could not leave a wounded man who needed care. He went to the telegraph key and banged away on it, but this time there was no chattering response, no sound at all. He tried again . . . nothing.

He took out the pistol and examined it, looking to the loading of it. After a time he figured the weapon out.

He walked from door to door staring outside, but there was nothing. It was hot and very still. He took off his black coat. It was growing shabby. He combed his hair in front of a piece of broken mirror. His hair looked black when wet down, but was actually a very dark red, something you couldn't see unless it caught the sun.

He wore a candy-striped shirt and sleeve garters. His arms bulged with muscle, the kind they could use out there, laying track. He wiped the dust off his heavy brogans and tried to brush his pants clean. Then he looked out the doors and windows again.

It was very hot, and very still. He stared toward the relative coolness of the cottonwoods, but dared not leave the station.

He looked down at the pistol he was wearing and strutted a little. If they could only see him now! If only Maire could see him!

He went back inside and rummaged about for something to read. He found a newspaper, several weeks old, and a book by Oliver Optic that was quite new. It was called *Brave Old Salt*.

He opened the paper. Advertisements for patent medicine, the Sioux on the rampage in Dakota, and somebody named Rowdy Joe Lowe had killed a man: his second, some said, others claimed it for his third. A young girl lost with two children . . . he tried the silent telegraph key again, but there was no response.

Walking outside onto the platform, he stood alone in all that vast and empty silence, staring along the tracks. His eyes followed the wires. As far as he could see in either direction they seemed intact, but he knew they had

15

been cut. And the notion began to grow in him that if you wanted to stop a train, then just to make sure it stayed put you'd tear up a bit of the track farther on.

Out of the tail of his eye he caught movement, and turned. Far out on the grass, a black dot. Then there were two . . . no, there were four . . . five.

They came in dozens then, huge things with shaggy heads. Big, black cattle they were, like none he'd seen before, and all matted from rolling in the mud. All day long they kept coming, some of them brushing against the shack, and when night lowered they just bedded down where they were, paying no mind to the building or the men inside it.

Little it was that Crispin Mayo slept that night, for the great creatures muttered and moaned, sometimes their horns clashed, and several times one arose to stretch and scratched himself so vigorously against the corner that the shack rocked on its base.

It was after midnight when the wounded man awakened, and Cris sat down by him. "It's all right now. It's a grand hearty lad you are, and you'll be up and about soon."

The muttering stopped, and clear and sharp the voice said, "Who is it? Who is there?"

"It's me. The Irish lad left behind by the train."

"Train!" His voice shrilled until Cris feared he would frighten the beasties out yonder. "It's the train they're after. It's murder they plan!"

He muttered, cried out loudly a time or two, and only the fact that the great herd of beasts was now lying several hundred yards away kept them from milling about and perhaps knocking down the little station.

Cris Mayo paced the floors of the two rooms. All was still. He was worried, knowing nothing he could do for the wounded man, and no way in which he could tell anyone of the trouble they were in. He could only wait for the next train to arrive and hope that the man would live that long, and that the bad ones, whoever they had been, would come no more. He sat on the floor, his back against the wall, but could not sleep.

Hours later he was startled by a shot. He lunged up

16

from the floor, then dropped to his hands and knees, groping for the rifle. Suddenly, some distance off, there was another shot, then a thunder of hoofs. He threw open the back door and by moonlight he saw them coming.

Rushing out, he waved the red lantern he had kept lit in order to stop any train that might come through, and he shouted. Then, drawing the pistol, he fired it at the approaching mass. A big bull went to his knees not thirty paces off, started to scramble up, but another shot dropped him.

Cris fired again, saw another stumble but recover. Waving the red lantern and shouting, he managed, with the help of the fallen bull, to turn some of them. Backing up, he paused at the door to fire again. He scored, and a second animal fell.

Holstering the pistol, he grabbed the rifle from its place by the door, and wasted at least six shots that had no effect on anything. A big bull leaped one of the fallen animals, hit the corner of the station with a shoulder, jarring it to its foundations, then charged on.

Again he fired, point-blank, but the beast crashed by as though Cris had but breathed in its face.

The herd thundered on, parted now by the fallen bodies as well as by the building. Cris fumbled with the pistol, reloading it. When he looked through the door into the other room the wounded man was up on one elbow. "What is it?" he asked.

"Those black cows. They rushed upon us after somebody shot at them."

The man lay back down. "Buffalo. They're buffalo. The building shook. I thought it was going." The man lay still, breathing hoarsely. "Who are you?"

"The train left me. I told you."

"Can you handle a key? We've got to send word."

"I can't, but it makes no difference. The wire's destroyed and silent. I think it was cut."

"Likely. Likely they've torn up some track, too."

"It was my own thought," said Cris. "Who is it behind the trouble? Is it you they're after?"

"No." He looked at Mayo, trying to make up his mind.

17

This man was a stranger, yet he looked like what he said he was. He wore a square derby, a shabby but neatly brushed suit, heavy brogans. Certainly he was no Western man. "They're a bloody lot of renegades. They're going to take the train. I heard some talk after they'd caught me in bed and beat in my skull, and thought I was dead." He paused. "They shot me out back there, when they found I was still alive, and dragged me a ways off to hide me. They want to kill somebody on the train, and I believe it's General Sherman."

"Why, is he important?"

"He is. And he led the march from Atlanta in Georgia to the sea, burned plantations, tore up railroads, wrecked the country; but it broke the back of the South and helped to end the war."

"Is he on the train?"

"They think so. He's supposed to be coming west. It's an inspection tour, or something of the kind."

The wounded man closed his eyes and lay still, thinking. There was nothing he could do, no matter how much he worried over the situation. If the wires were down . . . and he had heard no sound from the instrument . . . they were helpless. Nor had he any idea just where or how the renegades hoped to seize the train. He tried to run over the possibilities in his mind, and he was still thinking of it when he fell asleep.

Crispin Mayo went to the door and peered out. It was very dark. There were stars enough, and he could see the dark bulk of the two buffalo he had killed. They represented meat, and as he looked at the hugeness of them he thought briefly of what such a vast mound of food would have meant to him at various times in the old country.

There he would have known what to do, what to do about everything; but all was strange here. The menace of "they," whoever they were, worried him. He had no part in this fight, and wanted no part in it. They had tried once to kill the man within, and when they stam-

18

peded the buffalo they were probably meaning to wipe out all trace of the telegrapher and perhaps of the station. But what had that to do with Cris Mayo?

The few moments of mental clarity on the part of the agent had helped him none at all, and it was gradually coming to him that nothing was going to help. He was caught in the midst of something that could mean the death of him and of all those fine dreams of going home to Maire Kinsella with her pert nose and freckles.

Ah, those fine, foolish dreams! He had thought to return wearing fine clothes, with a great golden ring on his finger, and driving a flashy pair of blacks . . . he'd show them! Well, now he'd be lucky if he got out of this alive.

He would fight. Naturally he would fight. It was never truly in his mind to do anything else, however he grumbled over it. That was the only way he knew, and he looked at the great dead black beasts yonder with a kind of pride. He had fired at them, and he had hit them. At the same time a wary little something in his mind warned him that they had been coming in a mass and how could he have missed? *Be sensible, boyo,* he warned himself, *do you not be betrayed by a bit of luck.*

Morning came again, and with it a renewed sense of vastness, of the enormous dome of the sky, of the sweep of the endless grass bowing before the wind. He recalled his village in Ireland, which could be dropped into this grassland and lost. Indeed, the whole of Ireland could be lost here.

He backed away from the thought, and glanced around the shack's rooms, where things were small, confined, easily understood. When he looked outside, the sheer size of it all overwhelmed him, yet there was also the fact that the soil was good. He had run it through his fingers . . . you could grow barley here, or rye or wheat, and you could grow potatoes. . . .

He was looking at the wounded man when he heard the pound of hoofs coming. His pistol was belted on under his coat, the rifle stood by the door. He walked to

19

it, started to step outside, and then did not. Why let them know he was alone? Or that he was there at all, till it came to the moment of necessity?

There were three; unshaven, dirty-looking men, one of them in an ill-fitting gray uniform coat like those that (Mick Shannon had told him)' the Confederates had worn. They drew up a few yards off, seeing the faint smoke from the chimney. They looked at the dead buffalo in the space behind the station, and then one of the men rode a slow circle around the place. Mayo held himself out of sight, and waited.

Finally one called out, "Hallo, there!"

Mayo crouched near a window, watching them, but did not reply. They called again, and then one started forward, but another called him back.

". . . dying," Cris caught the one word, and then, ". . . you saw . . . got to be."

There was more talk, of which he could distinguish nothing, and after a moment the three turned their horses and rode away to the east. He watched them go, and only when they had been gone for several minutes did he rise from his crouch.

He found a butcher knife and went outside to cut up a buffalo. Butchering was no new thing, for at home in Ireland they often slaughtered and dressed their own animals. Inside, he hung some of the meat, then began frying a steak.

He scowled, trying to think what he should do. These men who had nearly killed the telegrapher-agent would surely kill him and Cris both, if given the chance, and perhaps anyone who was on the train, too. He knew nothing of Sherman, but they'd no right to gang up on the man. What could Cris do?

A thought came to him, and he puzzled over it, considering all aspects. In the heap of tools he found a shovel and a scythe, and went out across the tracks and cleared a wide space in the dry grass. In the center of it he piled some of that grass, then took a chance and went to the cottonwoods for small branches, bark, and dried wood. With these he prepared the makings of a fire. From a stack nearby he dragged some railroad ties

20

. . . sleepers, some called them. The roof of the shack had been covered with tar paper and there was some left, fragments and trimmings. He gathered this and took it inside, where it at least would remain dry if there were a sudden shower.

He lit several of the red lanterns, and kept them lit. The oil from one of the others he poured over his kindling, and some of the ties he placed near enough to throw on the fire once it started, if so be it that it ever started at all.

The place he had chosen for the fire was across the main line and the sidetrack from the shack—he did not wish to risk burning himself out—and upon slightly lower ground. From the window it was invisible.

He ate his buffalo steak and found it not at all bad. He went inside, but his patient was asleep. Cris Mayo sat down on the chair near the useless telegraph key and stared out at the empty plains, feeling lost and lonely. He was tired from nights with little sleep, worried about the hurt man and about the renegades. That they would come back he had no doubt.

Finally, bored with nothing to do, he pulled out the drawers of the desk and ruffled through the papers he found there. One of them was a map like none he had ever seen before, but finally he realized that it was a cross section of the roadbed, indicating, among other things, elevations. As he was about to push the map away, he saw something that stopped him.

East of the cottonwoods the railroad started to climb; and level as it looked, it actually had a definite grade. He recalled then that the locomotive had slowed some time before they reached the station, until when it passed the cottonwoods it was moving scarcely faster than a man could walk. From there on, according to the figures, the railroad levelled off for some distance.

If riders were going to catch up to a train and board it, that would be the place, where the train had slowed to a walk. He had no doubt they knew all about that and had planned for it.

There were soldiers to the east and to the west, and these renegades would know that once word reached

21

them of General Sherman being taken from the train there would be pursuit, pursuit far beyond anything ever tried on the Western plains.

So what then? If they were desperate enough to attempt such a thing they must be prepared for a fight, but undoubtedly they also had planned an escape. That meant they would need time, and that meant first that the telegraph line be put out of action, and second that the train be unable to carry the news, because of the tracks being ruined or the crew killed. This would give them perhaps a few days of flight, in which they might scatter to reassemble elsewhere.

He butchered as much of the meat as he could, then tying a piece of rope to the carcass he tugged and pulled until he had hauled it away out of smelling range. The other was too heavy, so he had to let it lie there for a time until he could find some other means to be rid of it.

Crispin Mayo turned again to the plains and stopped, staring. A rider with a led horse was coming toward him. The led horse dragged something behind it.

He stood waiting, standing very still. The rider came on toward the station, and he saw it was an Indian woman, a woman with a small child. The led horse dragged two poles behind it, the ends trailing through the grass. She drew up when she saw him.

She looked from him to the buffalo. "Eat," she said, indicating the child and herself.

"Sure," Cris said. "I got some grub inside."

For the first time he saw there was a man lying on a blanket across the poles, an Indian man. His eyes opened when Mayo came toward him and he made a slow move toward a tomahawk in his belt.

"Lay off," Cris said, waving his hand, "you'll not be needin' that. We got one hurt man already."

The woman had been watching him, and he turned to her. "One inside," he said, "hurt."

She took her baby from the saddle and dismounted. She started to build a fire and he shook his head, pointing inside. He waited while she went in; shortly she returned, cut meat from the second buffalo carcass, and

22

went back inside. Cris got a dipper of water from the well and brought it to the injured Indian.

After a cautious moment the Indian accepted it and drank thirstily, so Cris went for another dipper, and the Indian drank that too. There was a trough at the well and Cris led the horses to it. One of them had a bullet-burn across its shoulder.

The woman came out with some meat and gave a piece to the Indian. Cris did not know how to talk to her, so he simply said, "It is no good here. Bad white men come." She looked at Cris, and he said, "Bad white man shoot him," he pointed toward the shack, "leave him for dead."

She indicated the Indian man. "Shoot him, too. We do nothing. Shoot him, shoot at me."

"How'd you get away?"

"Run . . . hide."

"How far away?" he asked.

She shrugged. "Not far. Many men, many guns. They camp."

He sat down on the back stoop and mopped the sweat from his face. "They will come here, stop the train. They want to kill general . . . chief," he said. And then he added, as she seemed to understand, "The chief comes on the train."

The Indian man ate slowly, methodically, chewing every bite with care. The small Indian chewed in the same fashion, staring at Cris with great serious black eyes.

"You go?" Cris asked, pleading. "You tell white man what happened? You go west?"

She said something to the Indian and he replied in a rough, harsh-sounding tone. She shook her head then, and pointed to herself and the Indian and then south.

"West?" he begged again. "You tell the railroad men. The steam-wagon men. You tell the soldiers." He reached in his pocket and took out three silver dollars. "I give . . . you take word?"

She looked at the silver, then at the Indian. The warrior looked up at Mayo. "No take," he said. "You keep." He gestured the money away.

"You take it," Cris said despondently. "You buy present for little one." He handed the three silver dollars to the woman, then stepped inside. He was tired and hot and scared, and he wanted to be away from there. Why was there no train? Wasn't anybody even wondering about the wires that were down? What sort of daft country was this?

He took off his coat and hung it over the back of a chair, and hitched the six-shooter to an easier place on his belt. The Indian woman was taking more meat from the buffalo, and he found himself wishing they would take it all. He wished . . . ah, he wished he was back in Cork!

The day dragged slowly by. He went out finally and wrestled some of the railroad ties over and piled a rampart of them against the walls on two sides. The walls of the shack were no protection, for a bullet would go through them as through paper. The railroad ties were another thing. He worked for several hours, stacking ties, and then he was tired, and sat down, soaked with sweat, his hands raw from the rough, slivery wood.

Sometime during his working period the Indian woman had gone, taking her man and child with her. He wished he had tried to trade her out of a horse. He could ride well enough. He'd once had a job helping the groom on an estate near his home. He had ridden a lot on those big, handsome Irish jumpers they had fancied.

He fixed himself a supper of buffalo meat, bacon and beans. Then he made broth for the wounded man, who was awake but in bad shape. He fed him a few spoons of the broth and the man waved it away.

Suddenly Cris had a hunch. They had tried to kill the telegrapher, and when he seemed to be still alive they had started a stampede of buffalo, and now time was running out for them. If a train was to come at all, it must be soon. So they would try to destroy the place that night.

He cleaned up the dishes and settled down for the fight. If he had been alone he would have walked out of there, even if he'd known he'd die on the prairie. But he wasn't alone.

He waited, and nobody came. He took the rifle as soon as it was dark and scouted outside. He put his tar paper near where his fire was laid.

Cris Mayo was standing in the door of the little red station when a train whistle blew.

Chapter Three

He gripped his rifle and stared eastward. Far away, he heard the whistle again. Running across the tracks, he dropped his rifle and struck a match. It broke. He tried again, and this one fizzled out. He swore bitterly and struck the third match and thrust it into the dry grass.

The flame caught, leaped up, and hastily he added the tar paper. The flames curled around it and it began to smoke. The flames caught, crackled, leaped up, and the tar paper burned, sending up a column of black smoke into the night, visible in the early moonlight. He threw on the rest of it and then, snatching up his rifle, ran for the shack. Somewhere to the east he heard a pound of hoofs: east, but from behind the station. A bullet struck a rail as he was leaping across it and he heard its angry whine. At the same instant two horsemen swept around the building.

Cris threw himself behind the small embankment of the railroad, ready to shoot; but the riders circled the house as though intent on it rather than on him. Suddenly he heard a feeble yell from within, then a shot. He lifted the rifle but, not trusting his aim against a moving target, held his fire, hoping for a better shot.

He heard a door slam open, an angry shout, another shot. Then the horsemen came charging toward the track. Shifting sideways behind some brush and a pile of ties, he lay quiet. They rode up and one man leaped from his horse to put out the fire.

Frightened but desperate, Cris Mayo took dead aim at the man, who was not over twenty yards off, and squeezed off his shot. He felt the gun leap in his hands, saw the man knocked forward, falling to his hands and knees in the flames. The man screamed, and Mayo shot again . . . missed . . . and worked the lever on his rifle and held his hand, watching.

The wounded man rolled out of the fire, aflame and screaming, thrashing over and over in the grass. The other rider circled, gun up ready to shoot, but uncertain where the attacker was hidden.

The wounded man lunged to his feet, then sprawled headlong, the flames from his clothes catching the dried grass. The other rider's horse threw up its head and began to rear, then to pitch.

The rider was busy, too busy to shoot, and moving too wildly to offer a good target for Cris Mayo's doubtful aim. He wheeled and tried to come back to the fire, but the horse refused. The grass was now crackling with flames, leaping high. The wind was blowing them toward the railroad and around the small cleared area where Cris had built his own fire, and then along the track.

The column of black smoke was mounting now, and the railroad train was whistling as it came up the grade.

The rider at last steadied his horse. Very carefully, Cris fired. He saw the man jerk sharply, then race away. Not killed certainly, but scratched at least and wanting no more of what was happening at the station, he rode toward the cottonwoods and what lay beyond.

Cris got to his feet, fed three shells into the rifle, and walked back to the station.

As he stepped inside he saw his patient sprawled on the floor, arms flung out, half his head blown away. In his right hand he held a small derringer. Evidently he had opened the door and tried to help, and they had killed him from out there in the night.

Cris walked outside and looked down the track. He could see the train coming. He thought he also saw a flurry of movement around the rear cars. The train came on, whistling again. Slowly it puffed and wheezed into the station. The engineer leaned out. "What's wrong? Is the fire a signal?"

"It is that," Cris Mayo shouted, "and you'd best be

27

looking to your train. You've lost a passenger, I think, taken from you while the train moved."

"A passenger?" The engineer was startled. "What do you mean?"

"The man who was here, who operated the instrument, was killed that he could send no warning, and I am thinking they may have torn up the track for you ahead there, as well as cutting the wires."

The conductor was coming forward. "Here! What's wrong?"

The engineer explained and the conductor turned and said sharply, "I don't believe a word ot it. Who are you?"

"I am Crispin Mayo, from County Cork, left here by accident, and I give not a curse whether you believe it or not. If you'll haul your disbelief back into the train you'll find they've taken a man from you, and perhaps more than one. If you do not believe me, then be damned to you."

The conductor stared at him, his face reddening. "You're an impudent rascal. If I had the time, I'd—"

"I will await your time," Mayo hitched his pants, "be it today or a year from now. If you're of a mind to get your face punched bloody and black, do you be keeping the meeting. I'll not disappoint you."

"You'd best not talk that way," the engineer advised. "Sam here is a noted fighting man."

Cris said coolly, "Then I'll use two fists to beat him instead of the one I'd been minded to. Now, if you have finished your talk, you can see to the dead man in yonder, and to your passenger. You were carrying General Sherman?"

"Sherman? How would you know that?"

"They knew it. Or they assumed it. The operator in this place had a thought they were Southern renegades, planning to kill the general."

"Nobody stopped my train!" Sam said angrily. "And I'll be damned if anybody *could!*"

"They had no need," Cris said, irritated. "You were moving slowly enough for them to take him without your stopping."

For an instant the conductor stared, then he wheeled and started toward the train. At the same moment there was a cry from the last car, shouts, and running feet.

Cris Mayo turned his back on them. "He's a stubborn man, your Sam there, and a fool," he told the engineer, and walked beside him into the station.

The dead man sprawled on the floor, and Cris showed the engineer the signs of the head beating, the first wounds, then the last one. "I cared for him, though I'm no doctor. I sent an Indian that those devils shot to tell the railroad men west of here, but the renegades are a hard lot, and in force. They may attack your train."

"They'd be fools then. We've nearly a dozen armed men aboard."

"And they've several times that many, by what the Indian's woman said."

Men came running up, several of them in uniform, and Cris Mayo waited for them, feet apart, hands on his hips. An officer was first to reach the platform. "Quick! We must telegraph!" He caught the engineer by the arm. "Where's the operator?"

"Dead . . . and the wire is cut." The engineer was cool. "Ask him."

The officer turned sharply around to Cris Mayo. "I am Major Andrews. What's happened here?"

"They murdered the operator, and they cut the wires, and more."

"Who are you and what are you doing here?"

"I am Crispin Mayo, headed west to work on the tracks. They came back again tonight. There was some shooting. I killed one of them."

"You did? Where is he?"

Cris led them across the tracks to the still-smoking fire. The dead man lay on his back, his hands and knees badly burned, his face scorched.

A soldier who had followed them spoke up. "I know this man, sir. He's Eph Caldwell from Georgia, but he rode with the guerrillas . . . a bad one, sir."

Andrews stared down at the body, faintly curious. He offered no comment, nor had he needed identification. The man's surname was not Caldwell, but he *had* been from Georgia. Their families had been neighbors; Eph had been a bad lot, always in trouble, always a regret to his family. "Sergeant," he said, "get a burial detail. I want this man buried and a marker put on his grave."

He turned to Mayo. "What else can you tell me?"

Cris repeated the little he knew, then added, "They must have a camp close by, for they could not have ridden far, to come here with their horses as fresh and unsweated as they were."

"They would not be at their camp now," the major objected.

"No, sir, but they might have left something. If they wanted to kill General Sherman they would not carry him far. They would take him to some other camp, then, if the whole scheme is revenge, they'd take their time with him."

Major Andrews turned to the sergeant. "Post a guard, front, rear, and in the center, alert at all times. Engineer, detach your locomotive and go ahead a few miles to see if the track is in good shape; watch the telegraph line for the cut; then get back here fast."

"Sir?" Mayo interrupted. "That's a bad lot. They'll kill him. A few men on foot might—"

"Afoot? They'd get nowhere. They wouldn't have a chance. Besides, the man they have is a tough man, a good man."

"General Sherman, is it?"

"No, they don't have the general. They got the wrong man. They have taken Colonel McClean . . . but he was in Georgia with the general. He even looks like him."

Cris walked back inside. All that was very well, and doubtless important, but it meant nothing to him. This Major Andrews was in charge now and Cris had nothing to do but get on the train and ride to the end of the line.

He hesitated about the rifle and pistol. They had belonged to the dead man and Cris Mayo certainly had no claim to them, but neither did these strangers, and he had seen no home address among the papers he'd found in the desk. He would keep them himself until he could get such an address and return them. He took as

30

much ammunition as he could comfortably carry in his pockets and in the loops of the gunbelt.

He felt let down and used up. He had hoped that his fire would warn them of something amiss, and it had stopped the train but it had not saved the general . . . the colonel, rather.

The group now stood on the platform, watching the locomotive start down the track. The major was there, and the conductor. There were several others. Cris Mayo went outside and standing near the conductor he said, "I'd like a ride to the end of track. They've a job for me there."

"You'll buy a ticket if you ride my train," Sam said coolly, "I know nothing about you."

"Then I shall buy a ticket, but please . . . do you not forget our arrangement."

Cris walked away, anxious to be as far as he could from the man, yet as he left he heard the major speak. "After all, Calkins, the man did his best to protect railroad property."

"He protected himself. I'll have nothing to do with these shanty Irish. They are filling up the country, and they'll ruin it."

"Better not let the general hear you say that."

"The general?"

"Sherman is an Irishman. His father, if I am not mistaken, was one of those Irish immigrants. Sheridan is Irish, too."

Sam Calkins' face was red. "It makes no difference. They're a poor lot, fit to swing a hammer and little else."

"What was this 'arrangement' he mentioned?"

"Oh, the fool wants to fight me! I'll whip him with pleasure."

The major glanced after Mayo, and Cris heard him say, "The man's got fine shoulders. If he has the heart to go with them you may have your work cut out for you."

"Bah! Those stinkin' Irish can't fight! You come an' watch!"

Cris Mayo walked off by himself and sat on a pile of

31

ties. He had slept little and what he wanted most was to rest. Sooner or later, even if his Indians did not carry the word, somebody would come back to investigate and then they would send a work-train to repair the tracks. Then he would go on through with the train. He had money enough for a ticket, but there would not be too much left after that.

He heard boots approaching and he sat up, opening his eyes. It was Major Andrews. "Mayo? Don't worry about that ticket. I've told him you are travelling on Army business. We will need your evidence as to what happened here."

"Thank you, sir. It's a fine thing you've done." He paused. "Sir? They'll be killing him, you know."

"I think not, Mayo. More likely they'll make us pay for his return. Anyway, I have only six men and the train—not to mention the general—must be protected. And we've no horses."

The major walked away and Cris Mayo lay back on the ties. He was very tired. Yet as he closed his eyes, he remembered the men he had seen and the viciousness with which they had attacked the telegrapher, who was not even an enemy. That they would kill the colonel he had no doubt, and nothing was being done.

The responsibility for the train was not his; the major must think first of that, and of the passengers on it. But the colonel, he worried Cris.

Suddenly someone was near him again. He opened his eyes wearily and sat up. It was a girl. She was young, she was beautiful, she was obviously worried sick, and she was looking at him. "Are you Mr. Mayo?" she asked.

"I am that, miss."

"Mr. Mayo, would you help me? I'm Barda Mc-Clean, Colonel McClean's daughter."

"What is it that I could do?"

"Find my father. Or help me find him."

"Miss, you don't know what you're askin'. I'm new to this country. Now if it was County Cork, and if I had a horse—"

"I have a horse. As a matter of fact, two horses."

Cris got to his feet and hitched his gunbelt into place; running his fingers through his hair, he put on his hat. "You have horses?" he asked, skepticism in his voice.

"They are on the train. My father's horse and mine. We're enthusiastic riders and we were bringing them west, hoping to ride the broad new country."

"Does the major know that?"

"Of course. I suggested he send some men out, but he refuses to risk two men in Indian country, and says that only two men could do no good against the renegades, anyway."

"He's right, you know."

"Then you won't help me?"

"Now I said nothing of the sort! I simply said he was right. He's an officer, responsible for his men, and he daren't risk their lives so recklessly. I've been wishing for a horse, miss, but I'll not lie to you: we've small chance. If your father is not dead I think that he soon will be, and by going out yonder I might ride right amongst them. They are canny men, and they know the land, which I do not."

"I'll go alone then."

"No, I'll go. I'm a horseman. And if we can get one of the horses from the cars I'll be off to find them, although it's the divil of a place to look for them, it being so big and all."

"All right, come look at them in the moonlight and choose your mount."

Only two men were on guard, and both at the front of the train. They had orders to walk down the sides and back, but it was no trick to open the car after they'd passed, for the groom had already done so twice, and Cris eased the ramp to the ground, then led one of the beasts down. Barda held the mare while he went back, and when he reached the car door with the second horse she was in the saddle.

"No!" he whispered hoarsely. "We'll have none of that!"

She swung her mare away and he went up into the saddle and down the ramp with a thunder of hoofs that brought a shout from the guard. She was off across the dark prairie and he after her, and behind him more shouts and much fearful swearing. He would pray for their souls, in good time; they were likely lads but they certainly knew a lot of the King's English of the back-alley kind.

His horse followed hers when he let it have its head, and overtook her upon the prairie when she had slowed down. "Now where do we go?" she asked. "You are the one who must lead the way. I know nothing of this country."

"No more do I, which I've told you before! You'll go back, Barda McClean. Where I must ride is sure no place for a lady."

"You will need me," she said, "and it's my own father you seek. I *will* ride." She held something up in her hand and it was a rifle. "Don't worry, Mr. Mayo, I can shoot this."

Sighing, he led the way to the farthest tip of the cottonwoods. There would be no pursuit, for the major's men had no horses. When he pulled up, Barda came in beside him. "Why are you stopping?"

"We'll need daylight. I'm not one of these red Indians, but I expect we can follow the trail of so many riders, unless they split up. I've trailed sheep a time or two in Ireland, and once in a while a cow or horse."

They dismounted. Cris Mayo picketed the horses on the rich grass near the trickle of water and they sat down near the trunk of a huge old tree. "You better get some sleep," Cris suggested, "morning will come all too soon."

He took off his square-topped derby and leaned back against the tree, dead tired. He took his rifle across his knees, eased his belt-gun to where he could put a hand on it quick, and closed his eyes.

The enemy camp could not be far. In the first place they would not have wanted to waste strength in riding to the railroad, but would have tried to save their horses as much as possible until after the prisoner was taken. Cris guessed it must be within three or four miles, perhaps even less. He was equally sure that they would not be there now, but a man had to start somewhere. If they were lucky they would find a trail he could follow. He knew that as a tracker he was no Western scout, but he hoped for the best. He had an idea the enemy would head south . . . they would find more sympathizers there, more places to get food and information. The possibility that they would keep Colonel McClean alive more than a few hours was almighty slim. If Cris and the girl found his body, they'd go back to the train at once. Cris tried not to think of what that would do to Miss McClean.

Twice he dozed. He was not expecting attack or even discovery, and trusted to the horses for warning, but he could not sleep sound for the thinking. When the first gray light of dawn appeared he saddled up, led the horses to water, and awakened Barda. Even in the morning she looked good.

"Is there any coffee?" she asked.

He picked up his hat, shrugged into his coat. "No, miss. We came away from that railroad so fast we came without anything to eat. We'll just have to tighten our belts a notch. Will you mount up?"

"But I thought—!"

"No, you didn't, and neither did I. We just got these horses and rode off. We'll be lucky if we eat this week," he said mournfully.

She was appalled, speechless.

"Of course, it doesn't happen that way in the stories," said Cris, looking at her. "Nobody seems to eat much in the stories, and when they do, they just happen on meals when they need them. Out here in this land the only thing we'll happen onto is trouble."

She was very quiet after that, and Cris wanted it so, for he had thinking to do. He led the way toward the east, scanning the ground as he rode. There was no sense in just rushing off wild-like. Until they had some kind of a trail to go by, they must simply go slow.

The grass all looked the same. He couldn't see any tracks. Here and there were buffalo droppings and those

of smaller animals, maybe antelope. When they had ridden out a mile from the cottonwoods he turned in a
slow arc toward the south, scanning the country.

"You keep your eyes open," he advised Barda, "and
if you see anything movin', anything at all, you tell me.
I'll be studying the ground."

For an hour they rode. He saw occasional places
where the grass was bent over or pressed down, but
nothing he was able to identify. How could a man follow a trail in such a place? Barda after a long time
said, despairing, "Will we ever find them?"

"We will. I just hope it isn't too late."

"What can we *do?*"

"You just let that be, until we find them. What we
do will be depending on the situation." That was one of
the things his uncle used to say. It all depended on the
situation. You learned that in the Army.

The sky was scattered with puffballs of cloud. The
day was hot and still. The cottonwoods had faded into
the distance behind. Cris Mayo drew rein, removed his
derby and wiped the sweat from his brow. Barda came
up beside him. Her cheeks were flushed with warmth.

He looked the country over carefully. The prairie
seemed level but was not, for it slanted upward to the
west, ever so slightly. One could see it in the streams, or
rather, the little troughs where rain had run off.

The renegades would have camped near water. He
started the colonel's horse again and rode east and
south, studying the horizon. He followed a run-off pattern for something like two miles before he found a
stream.

It was dry, with caked mud in the bottom. He turned
down the stream bed and walked the horses along. He
was half asleep when suddenly they came upon tracks.
Several horses, ridden at a good speed judging by their
marks, had crossed the dry stream bed, and the trail
seemed to have been used more than once.

He had no confidence in shooting from the back of a
horse, but he took the rifle from the scabbard and held
it in his hands for the comfort of it.

The trail, once seen, was not hard to follow. They

had gone scarcely a mile when it turned sharply into a fold in the hills. Following a dim path now, probably made by buffalo, they went further, and suddenly the fold opened into a flat, grassy bottom. Down the middle of this was a line of trees. Already in the open, there was nothing for it but to proceed, and they did. The trail dipped down into a stream bed and almost at once came to a deserted camp.

Cris Mayo swung down. "Stay where you are," he said, "and hold my horse."

Leaving her, he walked on to examine the campsite. By the trampled earth and grass and the scuffed scars upon two trees he found where horses had been tied to a rope running between the trees. Judging by the distance and the condition of the ground, there must have been at least a dozen horses, and probably half again that many.

Say eighteen men. It was quite a few, and there might be even more.

There had been three fires . . . maybe six men to the fire if they did their own fixing. It needed no more than common sense to take him that far. Eighteen was about right, then.

He found three curious circles on the ground that he studied for several minutes before it dawned on him that the men had stacked their rifles, and the broken circles were the marks of the rifle butts in the dust.

He looked next at the fires. Taking up a charred stick, he stirred one of them. A few coals, still faintly alive, appeared. Last night, probably. Certainly no earlier than yesterday afternoon. He looked around, trying to learn more, but he could not.

"Get down, miss, and we'll rest a bit. The horses need it, and so do we." He led both animals to the small stream for a drink, then picketed them on the grass of the meadow just beyond the trees.

The sun was getting high, and the day was hot. She stretched out on the grass in the shade and he walked about, studying the camp. They had broiled meat over the fire on sharpened sticks, and they had eaten well, for he saw some pieces thrown away and not entirely consumed. In the bushes close by he found a bottle that had contained liquor, emptied and thrown aside . . . dead weight for them, a priceless object for him. Carrying it to the stream he washed and rinsed it thoroughly, then filled it with water and left it in the stream to keep cool while he looked around for something from which to whittle a stopper.

Finding some proper wood, he went to work, and while he worked, he thought.

The wires were down. The track was likely torn up. The rails might be put back in place and the train, or at least a part of it, gotten over. Or another train might come to investigate from east or west.

In other words, the renegades would have at least a two-day lead on whoever chose to follow. Cris Mayo had no idea whether there were other wires along which messages could be sent to head them off, but any such wires were more likely to end somewhere to the east, for the only line going this far west was the one along the Union Pacific tracks.

So they would be likely to ride south and west to avoid the inevitable pursuit. He lay back on the grass and slept.

When he awakened she was sitting up. "Are we going on? We've been here more than two hours."

"We are," he said. He led the way to the horses and tightened their cinches. They had been picketed within reach of the water, so had undoubtedly drunk what they needed. Barda swung into the saddle before he could reach to help her.

"There are no tracks south of this camp save those coming north, so we still haven't found their escape trail, but I figure they went southwest," he said. "That way they'll be farther from the telegraph."

"I don't think so," she objected. "They would go south and east." When he started to argue the point, she indicated the southwest with a gesture. "That's Indian country. My father told me all about it. The Indians there are very fierce, and enemies of the white man."

They rode on in silence, heading almost due south for

a time. Although Cris doubted that she was right, he hoped she was. It was little that he knew about Indians except the tall tales heard on the train and repeated by a few travellers home from America.

"They may have friends," Barda suggested; "they may be riding to meet them, or to hide on one of their ranches."

Suddenly, before Cris could speak, they came upon the tracks of a large group of riders, and followed these—for they aimed toward the southwest, as Cris had predicted. Through the sun-filled afternoon they rode. "You are from Ireland," she said suddenly.

"County Cork."

"Is it nice there? I've always heard Ireland was so green and lovely."

"It is. But there is little enough for a man to do there, and many seeking work. I had a good job but they took it from me."

She looked at him, and he explained. "There was a girl, a girl with freckles on her nose, and her father had plans for her and none for me. When some small troubles came, they used the excuse to be rid of me."

"Were you in love with her?"

He shrugged. "I can't say. She was a fine one, a pert, snippy one and good fun, too, and a grand time it was that we had together."

"Are you going back?"

He shrugged again. "How can a man tell what he will do? I am a poor man, and no fortune will come to me unless I earn it with me two hands. The hands and the will, they're all I have."

"And all a man needs, my father says."

The country had grown rougher as they rode, and the trail seemed fresher. What would he do with her when they came to the trail's end? Probably some fool thing on the spur of the instant. He was a rash one, as they had said back in Cork. But maybe this affair needed rashness.

"Where is your home?"

"Since mother died . . . four years ago . . . it has been wherever my father was stationed. In the Dakotas, in

Texas, and for a little while in Arizona. We're heading—at least we were—for California, after the meeting at Fort Sanders."

He led the way down a shallow fold in the hills, watching with interest the tracks on the badly washed slope. He found himself wanting to talk less and listen more, though he was mildly curious about that meeting she had just mentioned. He knew he was being a fool. There had been no reason at all for starting off into the prairie with this girl . . . only that she would have gone alone, and besides, Cris had felt that something should be done at once, while there was time.

He drew up suddenly, a twitch of his horse's nostrils stopping him dead. Cris now, as well as the beast, could smell smoke . . . faint, but there none the less.

"What is it?"

"Ssh!"

He heard nothing but the wind. The smell of smoke was vague now . . . did he really smell it? He waited, listening. Then he walked the horse forward, turning briefly to put a finger to his lips. The small draw took a sudden turn and the smell of smoke came stronger. Rifle up and ready, gripped in his right hand, he rode around the corner; the draw opened out and there were half a dozen trees, a few scattered rocks, two horses, and a man seated at a small fire.

He made no move to rise, nor did he lift his head from his chest. Cris lowered the rifle muzzle a few inches, but the man made no move.

Slowly, trying to hold the fellow in sight, Cris Mayo let his gaze take in the whole situation of things. Below and beyond lay open prairie, a hundred yards or less beyond the fire.

"All right! Who are you?"

The man did not reply.

"Crispin," Barda said, "I think the man is dead."

Chapter Four

The man's head came up. "I ain't nuther daid. I'm live an' fittin' as you."

Crispin Mayo, a cautious man, kept the rifle in position. "What are you doing here? We're trailin' some renegades, and here you sit, right on their trail."

"I was with 'em. They done took me, days and days ago 'twas, figurin' me for some kind of spy. I didn't see no reason to be spyin' on them. Then one of them 'collected knowin' me from way back. He'd knowed my folks in the mountains and said as much, so they didn't shoot me down, they taken me along and I made to go with 'em until they got all taken up with their prisoner . . . then I ketched them two horses last night, one of which was mine, and I lit a shuck for Georgia."

"Georgia?" Cris asked suspiciously, recalling what the telegrapher had told him of Sherman's cruel march there.

"In a manner of speakin'. For any place that was afar off. Then after a while I crossed their trail and camped on it, 'cause they'll never come back for me."

"Did you see their prisoner? Did you talk to him?" Barda asked.

"I seen him. He was some kinda sodger. A square-built, oldish man, carried hisself mighty well 'spite of the way they were treatin' him. They was sneerin' at him, callin' him 'William' and 'Tecumseh' and the like."

"They are thinking that he's General Sherman," Cris explained, "but they have the wrong man."

"They'll kill him. Sure as shootin' they'll kill him. I figure they want to burn him some before, but they'll

41

kill him." The man stood up. He was about thirty, very tall, and very thin, with high, slightly stooped shoulders and big hands.

"What you considerin'? Goin' after a pack o' lobo wolves of that kind with a woman along?" The tall man looked sternly at Cris, his expression deepening to a scowl. "If they lay hand to her she'll wish she'd never been borned."

"She wouldn't go back," Cris said. "I told her, but she would not."

"The soldier you saw is my father," Barda said.

"Makes it no different. Leave the huntin' and fightin' to the menfolks. That's an awful mean crowd yonder."

"Nevertheless, I shall go. I must help."

"Ma'am, you surely do make it difficult. I want no more of that outfit. They struck me poorly from the start, an' I taken the first chance I seen to get shut of them. Now you ask me to go back."

"I've asked you nothing of the kind!"

"Ma'am, you surely have. If you-all go, I can't keep to runnin', I just naturally got to help. Man can't do nothin' else. And I'm of no mind to."

"We haven't asked for help," Cris Mayo said patiently. "You go along now, or sit here by your fire."

"It ain't fittin'. I'm all made up to run and now you-all come along an' shame me. I'll go yonder with you, for better or worse." He paused. "My name is Reppato Pratt. I'm from the Highland Rim country of Kaintucky."

When they had made themselves known, Cris indicated the packs. "If you have anything to eat, we'd be grateful to share it with you. We've had nothing today but water."

"I've no choice but to feed you, I reckon. When I lit out of there, I taken unto me one of their pack hosses, carryin' what I could lift on him, an' most of it is grub. I taken some bullets, too, not being wishful of lacking lead for shootin'."

Reppato Pratt stirred up the fire and toed the coffee-pot further toward the coals. Taking out a huge hunting knife, he began to slice bacon into a skillet with

42

amazing dexterity. It spoke not only of his skill but of the sharpness of his blade.

"They'll be headin' for Cherokee country. Leastwise, so it seems to me. That's southeast o' here, Mick. But I don't figure they'll keep the sodger long . . . soon's they've had their fill of vengefulness and meanness, they'll knock him in the head."

"Who's in command?"

Pratt shaved a few slices of bacon, then glanced up. "Now I done some ponderin' on that, Justin Parley, calls hisself Major Parley, he shows up front most o' the time. But there's two others a body would have to take into account. One of them is a gun-handy killer called Del Robb.

"This Robb is a good-lookin' man and a mighty fine horseman. He killed a couple of men down in Mississippi and headed west. For a time he shaped around down by the Sulphur River in East Texas, but he didn't get along with Cullen Baker, Bob Lee and them so he pulled out and trailed west.

"He killed a man in Fort Worth, shot one up in Beeville but that one lived, and then Robb trailed around down on the Neuces for a spell. That's all gossip I picked up when I was a-settin' by.

"Parley, he takes the lead, but Del Robb is right there to hand, and there's some among 'em believe he's the power.

"The other one is Silver Dick Contego. They call him that because of his silver-gray hair. He's a slender, quiet man who has the beautifullest hair I ever seen on a man, and he combs it all the time. He's got him a funny, old-fashioned comb with a round back to it. They make no move without him, but he never pushes on anything or anybody. He sets quiet, but nobody makes much of a move until *he* thinks it's all right. Silver Dick is a friendly-seemin' man but something about him makes me uneasy, an' I don't know why."

As Pratt talked on, Cris listened hard, and the picture slowly unfolded of a body of men most of whom were former guerrillas from the Civil War; few of them had been regulars, and some were just a rough lot picked up

43

as they moved through the country, a band of cut-throats led by Parley with his two lieutenants. Such an outfit was basically unstable, usually held together by fear and greed.

He had known of such groups in Ireland. They often began as men fighting for liberty, and then the best of them pulled away or were killed and what remained were those who had lost perspective and thought only of murder and loot and their own image of themselves.

"You rode with them a time," Cris said. "How many are there?"

"Seventeen, but more are scattered 'round Fort Sanders, an' some comin' to jine up from Texas."

"Have you any idea where they'll camp the next two nights?"

Reppato Pratt considered that, then nodded. "I can figure one camp 'most for sure. Reason is, it's hid good, and there's plenty of water an' fuel. We stopped by there on the way up." He looked over at Cris. "You ain't figurin' to tackle them head-on?"

"No," Cris said, and a thought came to him as he spoke. "We must attack, we can't just sit back. But we can't take them by force, so we've got to be smart; hit them where it will hurt them most, and stop them from running. So we'll either steal or stampede their horses. Set the divils afoot."

Pratt nodded. "Now! Would you listen to that?" He looked over at Barda. "He pounced on the one thing we can do. We set 'em afoot and they'll . . . why, a man can't do anything in this country without a horse!" He considered. "Won't be easy. Won't be at all. They surely do guard them horses."

"You be pouring that coffee, and let us give the problem some thought. I want to know all that you know about that camp, and where they'll tie their horses."

Even as he said it, Cris was thinking that there were other things a man could do besides this one so hastily struck upon. The secret, his uncle had told him, was to attack, always to attack. The enemy was always vulnerable. Some place, invariably, there was a weak spot.

Steal their supplies? Set a prairie fire? Cut off their water supply? It was not the size of the force you had that mattered, it was how you used it.

Cris Mayo sat beside the fire and ate the bacon and drank the coffee, relishing every swallow as only a hungry man can, yet as he sat he was wishing he had the skills he'd heard that the old Indian fighters possessed, skills they learned from the Indian himself. He could have used many more skills than were at his command ... but of one thing he was positive, the first move must be against their horses. He must rob them of mobility, and then before they could recapture their mounts or get others, the cavalry might come. Or some other such miracle might occur, he thought wryly. At least, afoot, they might hold off on killing the colonel, for fear of the Army.

How he was to get the horses, well, he left that to the future. It all depended upon the situation.

Could he trust Reppato Pratt? He believed he could, but just the same he would ride behind. He told Pratt so as they put out the fire and prepared to mount up. "We don't know you, mister, so if you don't mind, you ride ahead with the young lady. I'll sort of trail along behind."

"Cousin, you jess do that! To ride beside Miss Mc-Clean is all anybody could be wishful for. I take it a privilege!"

Cris Mayo scowled. Damn it, what the fellow said was true, and why should he get all the luck and Cris none? However, he followed them a few yards behind, his rifle ready to hand. The trail was plain enough.

Over their meal Pratt had outlined the situation at the spring. It was in a hollow among low hills, whose rounded, grass-covered slopes were bland and innocent, and seemed to offer no route to anywhere in particular; there was a narrow, single-file trail that led through the bushes and into a small basin containing the spring, a few cottonwoods, and some willows, as well as other low brush. On one side of the small slough was a thick clump of cattails. There was an opening out of the

45

southwest corner through a cluster of cottonwoods, and it was near those trees that the horses would be placed at night.

"They let them graze?"

"That's earlier, but they take them through the trees for that and a couple of herders watch over them. They'll be in a long, low valley between the hills while grazing, and no way a body could get at 'em 'thout bein' seen. An' with that outfit, Mick, to be seen is to be shot . . . they don't figure to talk with anybody."

Cris was scared. He admitted it to himself, but he'd gotten in and he knew no way of getting out, not with the girl here, so determined and so vulnerable. Against the kind of men they faced they'd have only one chance, and they'd have to shoot first and straightest; and Crispin Mayo was only a novice at firing a gun. To relieve his feelings, he said stiffly to Pratt, "You'll do me the courtesy of calling me by my own name, or I'll have to lambaste you . . . which would be unpleasant, and you helping us so friendly and all."

Pratt chuckled. "All right. You call me Rep."

They had been riding for over an hour when the Kentuckian suddenly said, "Cris, you better give this a thought. That outfit ain't about to set still an' let us ride over the high prairie at 'em. They'll stick a man up in a cottonwood or atop a hill, and he'll see us comin' for miles."

Cris was irritated. That was obvious, and made him look the fool. He said, "Let's get yonder to the low ground, then."

Reppato Pratt led a winding way through connecting valleys among the rolling hills. Here and there was an outcropping of rock, and the land grew drier, the vegetation more sparse. Cris mopped the sweat from his face and shifted his grip on the rifle to dry his palms on his pants. Wouldn't be much left of his suit after this ride, and he had no other.

That was the trouble with being poor: a man could not make a move without thinking of the consequences. A man who had another suit or more than one extra pair of pants need only go to the closet or the wardrobe

46

and pick and choose; but a man who had no more than he owned now could never cease from worry that he'd be left without any. This eternal riding was playing hob with his pants, and soon he'd be out at knees and seat, with only one extra pair to his name and them maybe lost or stolen at the end of track.

Holding to low ground, they rode slowly forward. They'd have to attack by night. That thought came to Cris and did not worry him. He was no red Indian but he'd done his share of poaching, and could move quietly and easily in the darkness.

It was nearing sundown when Pratt lifted a hand to stop them. He dismounted and walked forward, studying the ground. They were beside a small stream that flowed toward a river, easily distinguished by the tops of trees, only a mile or two away.

Pratt came back to them. "Couple has been through here," he said, "scourin' the country, no doubt, to see if they're alone. Outriders."

"You think they'd come back?"

"Ain't likely. None o' that crowd's over-ambitious. They'll be watchin' the land, but we've raised no dust an' we've held to low ground so there's a blame good chance they ain't suspectin' they got company. Right ahead of here, I seen it, there's some cover an' a spring of water. We'll just set down there an' wait for nightfall."

They had not long to wait. Cris Mayo took off his coat and folded it behind his saddle. He knew that what lay ahead would be dangerous and he might not come out alive, yet he had no idea of quitting. He was scared and jumpy, of course, and low in his mind, but he'd not quit.

He wasn't hungry, and he should have been. The stars began to come out in the still-light sky, a soft wind blew through the leaves and the grass. He went to the spring, drank, then bathed his face and eyes in the cold water. When he stood straight, Barda was beside him. "Cris," she said, "I'm frightened." She looked up at him. "Are you?"

"I am."

47

"But you're going on with it?"

"I am."

"I got you into this. If anything happens to you I'll never forgive myself."

"Too late for that now, Miss McClean. We're in it. All three of us."

"I cannot believe this is happening to me. I cannot believe that those men would be as brutal as you and Rep say."

"Nobody ever believes it until it is too late. Everyone has the same idea: that it could not happen to *them*. It is always happening to somebody else, and you see it in the papers and don't credit it. Thieves, outlaws and the like, now, they are no braver than you, and most times less brave. They just figure you will be scared to a jelly, and will do nothing to defend yourself because you think they are so dangerous."

She was silent. He liked the nearness of her, yet he was no fool. This was a colonel's daughter and he was an immigrant laborer, a man with no future that anybody could see. Besides, back in Ireland there was Maire Kinsella. Yet Maire's features had faded somewhat in his memory, and that disturbed him, because it was Maire for whom he would one day go back to the old country.

"You're very brave," she said. "I will not forget what you are doing."

"If we get out alive," he said. "I am not all that brave, and they are better shots than me."

Reppato Pratt came softly down to the spring and drank. He got up, wiping off his bristly chin. "They'll be eatin' now, and soon they'll take in the horses."

Cris decided suddenly. "We'll go now. When they start to herd the beasts, we'll move."

Rep hesitated, then shrugged. Cris turned to Barda. "You stay close enough, and run with us when we run. We might not be able to get back here after you." Then they moved out until the enemy was in sight; and there they halted and watched.

The horse herd was three hundred yards or so from where they waited. The two men on duty were not mounted; shortly, they walked out to start driving the horses to the picketing site. The sun was down. The herdsmen were expecting nothing, and the horses began slowly, reluctantly, to leave the grass.

"Walk your horses," Cris whispered, "until they see us or we're within two hundred yards. Then let them have it!"

Steadily they went through the gathering darkness, that late twilight when all things become indistinct and shadowy. Cris held his pistol ready, and he spoke to the colonel's gelding that he rode. "Easy does it, boy, easy does it!"

The horses were beginning to gather, their heads pointed toward the narrow trail that led into the hollow where the outlaws were camped. "All right, now," Cris spoke just loud enough to be heard. "Let's *go!*"

His words ended in a shout and they slapped heels to their horses and charged, Rep's packhorse on a lead coming behind them. Startled, the outlaws' horses threw up their heads, nostrils wide, and saw four dark forms charging down upon them, the air ringing with yells.

Rep fired, and one of the herdsmen spun and dropped, staggered up, then fell again to one of Cris Mayo's slugs. The other man fled from what he evidently took to be a cavalry charge. Shouting and firing, the three riders raced after the fleeing horses. From the hill behind there was a shot, and Cris ducked involuntarily, having felt the whip of the air as the bullet passed, and then they were gone into the darkness, driving the horses ahead of them onto the vast plain.

He could not believe it. They had brought it off, and for the time at least the outlaws would be unable to leave. Far into the night they drove the horses, finally losing them as the herd began to lag and scatter. They made no effort to keep the horses bunched then, just let them go, confident that few would find their way back.

At the camp in the hollow Justin Parley waited for the report, and it could not have been worse. "Three or four riders," the lookout said, "and there might have been more. They got Wes Jackson with their first fire, an' Noble, he cut an' run."

"The horses?"

"Scattered over the prairie, every blamed one! We'll be lucky if we can round up half a dozen."

"Noble?"

"He's waitin'. Says he didn't have a chance. Swears it was the U.S. Cavalry."

"He's a fool and a coward. Get rid of him."

Silver Dick Contego glanced up from his coffee. "Give it some thought, Major." Whenever Silver Dick wished to be persuasive he always used the title. "Noble has kinfolk down yonder in the Indian country. He's half Cherokee, you know, an' we're ridin' right into his home base. They'll be askin' after him."

Parley hesitated only a moment. "Of course. We must not judge too harshly. By the time we reach the Cherokee country he may have given us reason to forget his error. In fact, we will give him a chance now. Noble?" he called.

The man was large, fat around the waist, heavy in the jowls. He was sweating as he walked forward, obviously frightened.

"You've allowed our horses to be stolen, Noble, but you're a good man. So good that you're going to prove it by going out there to recover them. Noble, I want you to leave now. Don't come back until you have at least four horses. With that many we can recover the others."

"But—"

"Now, Noble. This minute. I trust to your skill. Just bring them back to us."

The big man hesitated, trying to find words that would get him off the hook, but there were none. He turned and stumbled toward the second campfire, a desperate and frightened man.

The hawk-faced man who called himself Murray, squatting by the fire, spoke up as Noble came near. "Pete, you take a walk over that direction. That gray of mine, he surely did take to that grass at our last camp. He's apt to wander back there, and where he goes, others will."

Pete Noble nodded gratefully. "Thanks, Murray. I'll give it a try."

50

He walked off into the night, and Murray finished his coffee and stood up. Sometimes, as now, he wished he was back in Hannibal, loafing along the river front.

He considered Noble. The man was all but useless, so he had better go himself. He gathered some rations and extra ammunition, and turned to the men at the fire. "We'll *need* those horses. I'll have a try myself."

Let Pete Noble go on ahead; he would follow. Let Pete draw the fire. Pete would answer it while he could, and then Murray would get the horses.

"And then," Murray said aloud, "I'll—"

He let the sentence go unfinished, keeping his thought to himself.

Chapter Five

Colonel Thomas McClean leaned his shoulders against the stump. The ropes were tight and his wrists hurt abominably. His ankles, also bound, did not. The outlaws had tied the rope around his boots, and if they gave him a chance he thought he could slip his feet out and get away, but there seemed small chance that he would find the opportunity. He was closely watched. At least he wasn't tied to the stump.

Yet something had happened at last, something that gave him hope. The horses had been stampeded and temporarily the renegades could not move. To try to leave here would put them out on the bald prairie, visible and vulnerable to searching cavalry and prowling Indians alike.

He eased his position a little. He had told them repeatedly that he was not Sherman, but some of them believed he was lying. That they planned to torture and kill him he understood; facing that, any development could raise a man's hopes.

Yet he was puzzled. From talk in the camp—and nobody attempted to keep him from hearing—the horses had been stampeded by three or four white men. Who could they be? Not the Army, not yet. One of Parley's gang had been shot, and now they had sent the man Noble off into the night after their horses, with Murray following him.

For a day, perhaps even two days, they would not dare to move. He considered that. They had told him that the telegraph wires had been cut, which he had guessed, and that they had torn up the track; but those were only temporary setbacks. His orders had been to report on conditions at once. He was known for his efficiency and speed of action, so when no report appeared, authority would begin to move at once. The disappearance of the train would be investigated from both ends of the track, the seizure of his person discovered, and several troops of cavalry or Indian scout detachments would move out.

Within forty-eight hours, surely, the search would begin; forty-eight hours in which Parley and his renegades had hoped to escape into Cherokee country, where they could scatter and become hard or impossible to find.

The stampeding of their horses had been a shrewd stroke on somebody's part. Now they were immobilized and the situation altered.

The man called Silver Dick strolled over, tugged at the bonds to make sure they were secure, then squatted on his heels. "Don't get your hopes up. This is just a temporary delay. Our men will be back with the horses in no time."

"Perhaps." McClean paused, then said, "Contego, I wish you would consider the situation. You believe, as Parley does, that I am General Sherman. I am not. My name is Thomas McClean, my rank is that of colonel."

"You're wearin' a general's insignia."

"True. I was a brevet-general during the last months of the war, and that means, really, a temporary general. My permanent rank is only that of colonel. Actually, I am an inch taller than General Sherman and at least ten pounds heavier. My hair is darker than his. Only those who know neither of us well could mistake one for the other. The resemblance is superficial."

Silver Dick was thoughtful. "Then I suspect, if that's a fact, that they won't chase after you the way they would the general?"

"Wrong," McClean said. "Contego, the general is in command, and Sherman is not one to be laggard in such a case. I'd say that mounted patrols are already fanning out from a dozen positions, all of them hunting us. Partly because of me, but more, perhaps, because you stopped a train."

53

McClean eased his position a mite. "Contego, you are an intelligent man. Please consider your position. Nearly twenty-four hours ago, a messenger must have left the station to report to Fort Sanders and the end of track. There are forty-five soldiers at the fort, at least twenty at Hell-on-Wheels, and they can be detached . . . or at least most of them can.

"When my report failed to reach headquarters, inquiries will have been made, and certainly the telegraph wires will have been repaired shortly after that. At least four troops of cavalry, with Indian trackers, will be headed this way. North and his Pawnee scouts will also be out. You made a bold gamble, but you've lost."

"That won't do you much good," Contego said. "You'll be dead."

"I said you were an intelligent man, Contego. Dead, I am worth nothing to you. Alive, I could at least speak for the man who spoke for me."

Silver Dick studied him thoughtfully. He took out his fancy comb and ran it through his hair. "I'm not in command," he said. "Parley is, and Parley wants you dead. Del Robb wants *everybody* dead, or at least he doesn't care who he kills. We wanted Sherman. He wiped out some of our homes, he broke the back of the South. We got you. I believe you aren't Sherman, yes, but, I reckon you were with him, so we'll just have to give you what we planned for him, and catch up with him another time."

"Think about it, Contego. You appear to be a shrewd, careful man . . . why not have an ace in the hole? If you get away, you have nothing to worry about. If you are caught, I can always say you protected me. It might make the difference between hanging or not hanging."

Contego got to his feet. "Well," he said, smiling a little, "I'll admit one thing: that difference is considerable."

It must be almost ten o'clock, judging by the moon, which was full. By now it was all beginning to happen. McClean knew the machinery so well that he could picture every step. What he did not know were several things of importance to him.

He did not know that his daughter had been one of the three riders who stampeded the horse herd, or that miles to the west an Indian woman, her child, and her wounded husband were nearing Fort Sanders.

Nor did he know that only a few yards away from him, Justin Parley, Del Robb and several others were grouped together talking earnestly. "Suppose he ain't Sherman," one man was saying, "he's a damn Yankee anyway, so kill him an' bury him. Nobody can prove nothing."

"The girl saw me," another said. "I wish we had her here."

"I wish we had her, too," the first man said, and chuckled.

Parley tasted his coffee. It was lukewarm. Irritated, he put the cup down. "Who's after the horses besides Noble?"

Robb said, "Murray follered him. Noble ain't much good, but Murray's tough and he's mean."

"Noble's a good tracker," Parley said, "that's one reason I let him go. He may be a slob, but he's good at trailing, and he has no place to go unless he finds the horses."

"What about *him?*" Robb said, thumbing in the colonel's direction. "How long are you going to keep him around?"

"What's the hurry?" Silver Dick said mildly. "We've got him. Let's wait until we have some horses. If they should close in, we can trade him."

"That makes sense," Parley commented. He considered it. "The longer we keep him the more he'll worry. He isn't going to get away."

Pete Noble found the trail of the horses and walked along studying the tracks by the vivid moonlight. "Bunched," he muttered. "This ain't goin' to be easy."

Yet within the first mile he had isolated the tracks of the horses ridden by the unknown enemies, and had identified the prints of Reppato Pratt's horse, as well as those of the horse that Rep had stolen from their herd. Recognizing a horse's hoofmarks was no more difficult for him than for a bank teller to establish the authenticity of a signature, and he grunted with satisfaction. "Shoulda killed that Pratt," he muttered, "knowed that all along."

The other two horses were strange, both well-shod, and one of them with a long, swinging stride that ate up distance. He was envious. That was a horse! The fourth, which he soon knew to be a mare by its method of urinating, was also a fine animal.

Not many Western men rode mares, most preferring geldings; but this was a mare and ridden by someone of light weight. He had a hunch then, but it seemed so preposterous that his mind would not accept it. A woman? Not likely. Not in this country.

Pete Noble did not like to walk, but he could. In the country he had come from, walks of fifteen or twenty miles were not uncommon, and he had walked the hills many times, hunting. Luckily, no Indians seemed to be about and he strode on, making fairly good time.

The riders were not Indians, and the two strange horses had been freshly shod. There was no blacksmith nearer than Fort Sanders to the west, and not toward the east for at least a hundred miles. Hence, these horses had been shod some distance away, yet had been ridden no more than a few miles since then, for there was no sign of wear in the occasional sharp hoofprints he found.

He puzzled over this for awhile until the obvious solution occurred to him. These horses could only have been on the train. There had been a stockcar but they had paid no attention to it, being interested only in the car in which General Sherman was supposedly travelling.

Noble paused to mop his brow. Only *two* horses? Unlikely. Then there might have been a troop of cavalry, or maybe a squad, riding that train further up! Of course, there had been some soldiers, they'd seen them as the train passed, but had not suspected that there were horses too.

The conclusion to which he came was logical enough. There was a body of cavalry already on the trail of Parley and his men.

He was tempted to go back and warn them, but he had been told not to return without some horses. Moreover, if the cavalry caught up with Parley, Pete had no wish to be around. All Parley's men scoffed at the Army but none of them wanted any part of a pitched battle with a bunch of seasoned Indian-fighting cavalry; least of all, Pete Noble.

It was nearing midnight before he reached the point where the horses had scattered. He searched around until he found the track of Murray's big dapple gray and began trailing it and the half-dozen horses that accompanied it. The dapple gray was leading off, as Murray had suspected, toward their previous camp, for there was water and good grass there.

Shrewd as he was in the way of trails, Noble never suspected that he himself was trailed. He walked on now, sure of where he would find the horses. He would reach the place early tomorrow morning, allowing for a little rest now and again.

The three ridden horses with the lightly laden packhorse had left the herd shortly after the bunch broke up and began to scatter, but they were not his problem. Not now, at least. They had turned off toward the east, riding close together. There was a river over there, and they might be headed for that. They worried him little, for he would see them some distance off in the moonlight and there were buffalo wallows, crevices between rocks, clumps of brush, dips in the land, many places that would hide a lone man until he could bring them under his gun. And he was good, very good, with a gun.

Reppato Pratt led the way to the wooded valley near the river. "Ain't no way wise to huddle up close around no spring or on no riverbank. Not if you're on the dodge. Git what water you need and git back into close brush, where you can move several ways if need be."

Cris listened with respect. He was in command here, he told himself, but he was no prideful fool and he recognized when somebody knew more than he did, and he was not only ready but anxious to learn.

"We got to keep sharp watch," Rep said. "They'll be huntin' their horses and they'll likely foller streams, knowin' the horses'll want water. Some of the critters are prob'ly headin' back to their last camp, for it was a fine place to run stock."

"What would they do if they found us?" Barda asked.

"Now, ma'am," Rep said, "you've no need to hear the answer to that. They'd shoot us if'n we didn't shoot first." He looked over at Cris. "You done pretty good with that weapon. You used it much?"

"No, never. I just shoot where I look."

"Ain't no better way. You point your finger at something an' you're pointin' right at it. You been doin' it for years. It's the same with a six-gun. You just point an' shoot. The more you study on it, the more likely you are to miss."

He stopped his horse at the river and let it drink. "Rifle-shootin' when you're settin' off some distance, then you got to draw a fine bead. Use that sight, settle down an' take a mite of time."

When they had watered their horses they moved back into the trees, and settled down to rest in a small clearing. "No fire," Rep said. "We ain't more'n four, five miles from 'em now."

Cris took off his hard square-topped derby and placed it on the grass beside him. He removed the black coat, which he had not shucked in a full day and more, and adjusted his sleeve garters comfortably and tucked in the tail of his shirt.

Pratt looked at him in amazement, for his shoulders and arms bulged with muscles under the striped shirt. "Man, what are you? A rassler? You ain't carryin' a pound of fat on you."

"Me? I just worked hard. Farm work and fishing. Lifting, plowing, cutting the turf. I've wrestled some, and used me bare knuckles a time or two. I never had much time for setting about. It is fine land, in County

58

Cork, but there's much work to be done, many nets to be cast and drawn; and little time there is for standing about."

He had been cutting and loading turf when he was eight, and every year since, and he had drawn nets from the deep water from that time too. Besides, his family had run to big bones and muscles, and he had been the strongest of them all, and of his village as well. By the time he was fifteen he had thrown every man who considered himself a wrestler in all the county around, and at seventeen had thrown a famous strong man from Wexford, and then another at a fair in Mallow who'd claimed to be champion of Donegal.

At eighteen he had whipped a pugilist they brought down-country from Dublin, and the following year, one from over the sea in Liverpool. He had a natural, easy way with his body, and understood his strength very well; and his uncle had taught him much about leverage and the importance of placing the feet. At nineteen he suffered three defeats in a row from a Cornish-style wrestler who possessed skills he had not heard of, but the fourth and fifth time they wrestled, he won.

He examined a long tear in his shirt. He had but two others, provided that he ever found his things again. And he had very little money left.

They dozed and waited through the long dark hours, and hands behind his head, Cris looked up at the sky and squinted at the patterns the stars made. Barda came over and sat beside him.

"Where's Rep?" he asked.

"Asleep, I think." After a pause she said, "Cris, will we be able to get my father away from them?"

Cris shifted uneasily. "Maybe the Army will come," he said. "We've stopped them for awhile, anyway."

"They'll kill him, Cris. We've got to get him away."

"From sixteen men? You don't know what you're sayin'. It was a lucky thing we did, driving off their horses and not getting shot for it, but to get him from their camp . . . you're daft, girl. Daft."

"Mr. Pratt will do it for me, then."

Cris bristled. "He will, will he? He can do little that I cannot do, and believe me, a man would be a fool to go against them. A fool."

"You'd let them torture my father? Kill him?"

Cris twisted around angrily. "You are out to have us killed, Barda McClean, to help a man we do not even know. There are *sixteen* of them!"

"That's not so many!" she said pertly. "I've read stories where—"

"Stories, is it? I'll be telling you once more, girl, that this is no story. Nor are their guns shooting paper bullets, nor words, either. There's death in them."

"You mean to let him die then?" she asked scornfully.

Deliberately he got up and walked away without answering her, repeating in his thoughts the angry words he wanted to say but would not; yet even as he did so, her taunt disturbed him. Suppose Rep did do it? And he might. The backwoodsman was a daring man. He might even have friends in their camp.

Irritably, he went to the four horses, checking the ropes that picketed them, listening to their teeth tugging at the grass. The colonel's horse turned its head to brush him with its nose, and he rubbed its neck and muttered to the horse in Gaelic. Certainly, the horse was quick to respond when he spoke the language. Could it be an Irish horse? If he ever met McClean he would ask him . . . if he ever met him.

For a moment then he felt an icy chill. The colonel was only a few miles away, perhaps about to be tortured and killed. And the man could have little hope. Of course, the Army was likely to find some of those who killed him, but it would be small pleasure to think of that, with him gone.

Cris Mayo recalled the disdainful eyes of Barda McClean. The girl is a fool, he told himself, an innocent fool. What does she know of such men?

He knew. He had seen cruelty in his time, had seen men murdered, tortured even, white men killing other white men . . . and for what?

Suddenly he turned swiftly, caught up the saddle blanket, brushed it off and threw it over the back of the

60

astonished horse. Then the saddle and bridle. He took up his rifle and he swung a leg over the big horse. All right, the girl was a fool, and so was he a fool.

But he would go, he would go now.

Chapter Six

Cris Mayo had never thought of himself as an especially brave man. On the other hand, he knew he was not a coward. Many times in his life he had faced danger: with the fishing boats far at sea, on the ship that brought him to America, and even in bitter fist fights in his own country; and he had always done what needed to be done. He had often been afraid, but he was used to simply going ahead in spite of the fear.

Now he rode quietly out into the night, making no sound, and saying nothing to Rep or Barda, not even looking in their direction. Once out of the trees and on the prairie, he rode swiftly toward the encampment of the renegades.

When he believed he was still at least a mile from his goal, he slowed down. He watched his horse's ears, knowing that they were his best guide to what was happening out there in the darkness. Swinging wide a little, he walked his horse forward, wanting the enemy to hear no pound of hoofs on turf.

Several times he reined in and listened. He had no idea of what he would or could do, only a vague hope that when he arrived, he might see something of which he could take advantage. He hoped also that with no horses to watch, their guard would be less alert.

He drew up finally, having circled close to the opening through which they had taken their horses at sundown. He mopped the sweat from his brow, for despite the chill of night, he was sweating. "You're scared," he told himself, "and scared you've a right to be, and if you knew what would be happening before this night is over, you'd likely be even more scared."

Near the foot of the hill he investigated a lone patch of brush and scrub trees that appeared to offer little if any concealment; but within it he found a hollow, maybe a dozen feet long and half as wide, where the earth had been gouged out at some far distant time. Here he left his horse, tied to the thick stem of a willow. Easing out between clumps of scrub, he paused to listen. Poaching had been good experience for this, for gamekeepers in Ireland were alert, ready to pounce on those who grew careless.

To go up the bald face of the hill was not a thing to which he looked forward, but there was no other way except through one of the two entrances, and first he must learn something of what lay within. Keeping low, he started up the hill. The grass was no more than five or six inches high, but there were occasional clumps of prickly pear, some boulders, and enough cover to offer an illusion of security.

At the top of the hill, easing to the farthest possible point, he looked over. Only one fire was still alight. Two others had burned down to coals, and around them he could see the dark forms of sleeping men. Three men bedded a little to one side would be, he decided, the leaders of whom Reppato had spoken.

He stared down at them, wondering what he was doing here. He had come west to work, to earn money, to build a life for himself, so how did he come to be here? Was it only the girl? That he feared for her? Or was it something else in him that pushed him into trouble? He had moved like this before, suddenly and on impulse, without thinking ahead, and it was no way to do.

He studied the layout below. Not much chance to get in there, not if he also wished to get out. The more he looked at it, the less he liked it. Nobody was going to go through one of those openings without being seen. And to go up or down the slopes was to be in full view of the camp.

He supposed he should be inventing some shrewd way of tricking them so he could get the colonel free, but he could think of nothing. Yet he was restive. He had come here to do something and he did not want to go back without at least a try. He felt sure Reppato Pratt would have come up with a plan.

The moments passed. He worried about the gelding waiting in the brush down there. Suppose it whinnied and they heard it? Or some animal came along? There were wolves, he'd heard, and panthers.

A man suddenly appeared, a rifle in the hollow of his arm, strolling toward the fire. The man bent over, added a couple of roots to the coals, then stood there, looking about.

The guard from the opening where the horses had been taken out, Cris supposed. Then if he was here, there, by the fire—! The opening was unguarded for just that long. He started to move, then stopped. The man was walking over to the prisoner, and he bent over him as if to test the ropes that bound him, but in that instant, Cris saw the flash of steel in the man's hand.

Was he going to kill the colonel? Cris moved his hand to his gun, but before he could decide, he saw firelight flicker on the knife-blade, then saw the man drop to his knees and the light caught the blade again. The guard was cutting McClean free. Now he was helping him up.

They turned and just enough firelight and moonglow touched the man's face for Cris to see that it was Reppato Pratt!

How in—?

He was helping the colonel toward the entrance when suddenly from behind them appeared the other guard. "Hey!" he called. "What's the idea?"

Rep turned swiftly and shot him, firing from the hip. And in an instant the camp exploded into action. Men leaped up. Somebody shouted, "McClean! Where's the colonel?"

Cris Mayo, settling his rifle against his cheek, knew the time had come for action. He opened fire.

His first shot was at the yelling man, and the bullet burned him or scratched him. The man jumped back, stung, and Cris fired again. That slug caught a man with a pistol in his hand who was knocked back into the fire. He screamed, leaped up, kicking over the coffeepot, his clothing ablaze. He staggered and several men rushed at him to put out the flames.

Cris tried a quick shot at the place he believed Parley to have been lying, and then fired again and again.

A bullet nicked a rock near him and whined angrily into the night. Rep and McClean had disappeared, and Cris decided it was high time he did also. Backing swiftly from the crest, he sprang to his feet and raced headlong down the hill, slowing only near the bottom so as not to frighten his horse.

The gelding was startled, head up, eyes wild. "It's all right," Cris said softly, patting the horse. "All right now," and he whispered a few words in the old Irish.

Prudently he took time to reload his gun, then untied the gelding and mounted. He rode out of the bushes, circled away, and listened. He could hear an angry murmur from beyond the hill, too far away and cut off by the hill to be distinguished. He walked his horse in the direction he suspected Rep would go, but heard no sound . . . nothing.

He turned then and rode back to their camp. All was still. He listened, moved carefully forward, every sense alert.

The camp was empty. They were gone.

Where was Barda McClean? Had she gone with Rep after her father? And if so, where were they now?

He led his horse to the water, then drank himself. He was puzzled, unwilling to believe that Rep would take Barda with him on such a mission, yet understanding how difficult she could be and how hard to leave behind.

He sat on the bank under the trees and waited, listening. The moon was down. He dozed, awakened, dozed again. Nobody came.

The sky grew faintly gray, sunrise was coming. He got up and walked back to their camp, some twenty yards from where he had been sitting . . . nothing.

He climbed the hill to look out over the prairie, but the vast plain, broken by occasional rolling hills, was empty.

What would the renegades do now? Attempt to recover their prisoner, no doubt, as well as their mounts. And to be revenged on those who had thwarted them.

He walked back to the camp, then stopped, suddenly, looking at some tracks. Not only tracks, but cigarette stubs. Two of them. Cris smoked but rarely, and then a clay pipe, and he had not seen Pratt smoking. Yet somebody had stood there, for there were marks of a man's shifting feet, rolling and smoking at least two cigarettes while he waited and watched.

Cris squatted on his heels, studying the tracks. A large man, worn boots, run-down heels, and a crack across the sole of one. Standing up, he looked through the willows at the spot that the man must have watched. Right before his eyes was where Barda had slept, or sat. He had chosen it for her himself as the most comfortable place to rest.

Suddenly, Cris was desperately worried. He had slipped off, saying nothing to anyone, and then Reppato Pratt had evidently done the same thing! Believing Cris Mayo was still close by, he had gone off to try to rescue the colonel, unknowingly leaving Barda alone.

Carefully, Cris studied the ground, but could make little of what he saw. The tracking he had done in Ireland had been little enough, only the deer he poached and an occasional lost animal. It was easier just to ask farmers or travellers if they had seen a lost animal than to attempt tracking it, except on the uplands.

The main thing, he supposed, was common sense. Men are far less inventive than they assume and whatever means they use to confuse a trail have inevitably been used before. And this man who had captured Barda McClean had probably not expected pursuit.

So what then? Who was he and where had he gone? Not back to the camp in the hollow or Cris would have seen them; where else? The lone man was probably one of the renegades, but not necessarily so. Assuming that he was, then the man had evidently decided to keep Barda to himself, or perhaps to ransom her by appealing to the railroad for money. This, Cris decided, was likely. There was little loyalty among such men as Parley had gathered about him, and each was out to grab as much as possible.

The morning was dull and gray. Cris felt restless, irritable, not knowing which way to turn yet eager to do something. He tried to follow the tracks of the man across the clearing, but failed. He circled warily, keeping an eye out for trouble but seeking any mark on the ground that might give him a clue. Finally he went to his horse, mounted and walked him outside the camp. From the hill where he had been last night, a man with either very good eyes or a glass would see him, but he did not care. It was Barda he was thinking of. Barda was in the hands of this unknown man, and must be found, and at once.

He came upon the tracks suddenly and no credit was due to skill, simply to his patience and effort. They were the hoofprints of five horses, bunched well together, the tracks of one of them sunk deeper than the others. This he could interpret. A man had captured five of the scattered horses, was riding one and leading four of them. Cris started to ride on, then on a hunch turned and followed the trail of the horses.

It took him only minutes to discover that it was this man who had found Barda alone. He had seen something ... perhaps Rep or Cris leaving the area ... and he had investigated. Then he had either moved in, or waited until the second man was gone. The latter, probably, thought Cris, recollecting the two cigarette butts.

Near the place where the horses had been tied he found the big man's track and he also found the smaller, sharper cut of a heel into an earthy space between clumps of grass ... Barda.

All right, then. The fellow who had found the horses had also discovered Barda, but he had not gone back to the camp of Parley's men. Searching about, Cris found the tracks leading off toward the west, and holding to low ground. Six horses now, one of them Barda's mare.

He reined in and studied the land he must cross. He was gradually getting the feel of the country, learning to see, hear and sense better than he had. The railroad seemed far away now; beyond all reach, as far as County Cork.

His eyes took in the long sweep of the hills, the westward way. Touching a heel to the big gelding, he started off at a spanking trot. He carried the rifle in his hands, and the trail of the horses was easily followed.

He had one advantage, he thought: he knew his ignorance. That meant he should go slow until he saw the right move to make, then he must move fast and hard. So far he had done nothing, except that he'd opened fire to help Rep and McClean escape . . . if they had. Barda had been taken and the fault was in part his. He was out here, miles from anything familiar, following a man, who probably knew things he would never learn, into an unknown country. He decided that he was almost due south of the small red shack where he had left the train. By now there should be troops in the field, although it would take them awhile to get into this area.

Parley would be aware of that, and he also probably knew by now that his only chance was to find horses and get out of the country; so he and his men would leave their camp and march out to wherever they could expect to acquire horses.

The man who had Barda was holding a little south of west, and Cris Mayo stepped up the pace. He could go faster than a man with four led horses could go; unless that man chose to switch mounts, which so far he had not done, not knowing he was pursued.

The country was changing, the hills were higher, there were far more outcrops, and there were trees on some of the ridges. The land was drier, the vegetation stiffer, harsher, more gray than truly green. There was no difficulty with the tracks. In fact, when he topped out on a rise he could see them pointing a finger, a whitish streak across the mixed grass plains before him, pointing toward a rocky hill several miles off.

The man might be watching from over there but Cris decided he had no choice. He put the gelding into a gallop and started out for the hill.

Pete Noble was in a quandary. He had found the

horses where Murray had suggested he might, and he had started back. He was within a couple of miles of the rendezvous when he saw a rider come out of the hills and start across toward their hideout. No one in the outfit had a horse like the one he saw, a splendid animal.

There was a good chance the man was a spy, and there was an even better chance that a force of men lay in waiting yonder where he'd come from. Pete decided to scout the area before returning. This was something Parley should know.

He was nearing rapidly when he saw the second man leave, leading a riderless horse, and now he was more than ever sure. This was a military detachment or a civilian posse. In either case, Parley must know, to avoid surprise.

Leaving his horses, Pete had closed in carefully. Although a big man he was half Cherokee, had spent much of his life among Indians, and could move with great skill and silence. He was not a brave man but he trusted his skill and so was not particularly afraid of being caught.

Then he saw the girl. She was lying down. He got a glimpse of her face in the vague moonlight and knew that she was young and attractive. He mopped his brow and upper lip. A girl . . . alone?

He rolled himself a smoke and lit it carefully, shielding the flame, as soon as he'd determined that she was alone. Only one horse was tethered nearby, a mare. Pete Noble thought hard, through that cigarette and then a second. Two men gone, one girl left. . . .

She had been one of the three who drove off their horses! Justin Parley would be glad, and grateful to Pete, to have her a prisoner.

Parley? Why let *him* have her? Why not keep her for himself? He'd found her, not Parley. And who was Parley after all? Pete Noble did not need Parley. He had lived in the West for a long time before Parley came into the country. Half of his ancestors had lived here forever! Suppose he took this girl and ran with her? Who was to know?

He moved into the small clearing. The girl's eyes flew open. "Ma'am," he said, "if you yell I'm liable to shoot you."

Barda McClean was frightened but she also knew that she dared not give in to her fright. She sat up. "Why should I yell? I know you've come to guide me back to the railroad to receive the reward."

"Reward?" Noble was not the brightest of men, but he knew the smell of money. "What reward?"

"Why, the reward the railroad is offering for anyone who brings me back, or my father. I am Colonel Mc-Clean's daughter."

Chapter Seven

Pete Noble turned the matter over in his mind. Thinking had never been one of his attributes, and he was worried over the problem. He had a girl here, a girl such as he had never had in his life and would never be likely to have again.

On the other hand there was the reward. He knew of no reward, but of course he had been nowhere to hear of it, and it was likely that one *had* been offered. He was no fool and he realized well enough that Parley had been on the verge of having him shot. Parley had men killed for less than Pete had done.

So why go back and risk Parley's displeasure? Why not take this girl to Fort Sanders and pick up the money? In fact . . . why not tell them where Colonel McClean was? That would mean even more cash.

Barda could see the man was fretting over a decision and she said no more. Her eyes scanned the dark hills as they rode west, hoping for some sign of Rep or Cris. There was nothing. No matter what this man might decide, she knew that she was in trouble.

"My father was scheduled to be at Fort Sanders on the 23rd," she said suddenly. "There is a meeting there of Generals Grant, Sheridan, Sherman, and Haney, with Thomas Durrant and Dodge and some others. It has something to do with changing the route the railroad is following. So you will have no trouble getting your reward."

The gray morning dawned.

He said nothing. They rode on for several miles in utter silence. As they turned around the base of a hill, she took the chance to look back, but she saw nothing.

Her hopes fell. Ahead was a long, dark grove of trees; for the first time she felt real fear. This man was not only huge, but gross, more animal than man, and she had no weapon with which to defend herself.

Obviously the man knew where he was taking her, for it was a bowl-like hollow, walled around with rocks, and open only on the side toward the river. There was a spring there, trees, fuel, and good grazing for the horses. In the bottom of the hollow lay about forty acres of good grassland, and Noble led the way toward a ring of stones on one side. The ring was filled with the charred remains of old fires.

Dumping her on the grass, he led the horses to water. There was no sense trying to escape, for he would track her wherever she went. Her one hope was to keep the idea in his head of taking her back. She sat herself up slowly, her hands careful.

He was dangerous, dangerous because he was slow, dangerous because there would be something in him beyond the reach of reason. He had strength. She was not a small girl and he had plucked her from her mare's saddle as if she were nothing. It was a heavy power, yet he was cat-footed when need be, she had seen him move a couple of times with incredible swiftness, so she must keep him on her side. And he was . . . almost.

She must not confuse him with too many ideas, or dull their edge with talking. He had her now, he could have a reward by delivering her unharmed. This was enough for the moment.

She had lived around Army camps much of her life and knew what life was about; she also knew that the respect of men was something easily lost. She had this man's respect now, for she had moved carefully. She was a colonel's daughter, and she must never forget that.

When he returned he began to put a fire together. His movements were smooth and without fault. This was something he had done many times, and there was no waste motion. She knew what he had been thinking by his first question. "What you doin' out here, any-how?"

"I was travelling with my father. He had business at Fort Sanders, as I said."

"I mean out here . . . on the plains . . . with them two fellers."

"I was looking for my father. I do not know one of the men, he met us out here." Then she lied for the appearance of it. "The other one is a railroad employee. I told him that if he didn't come with me I'd have him discharged."

He considered that. Bringing a few articles from his pack, he began to make coffee. Then he sliced bacon into a pan. His thick hands were dirty, but she knew she must not notice and deliberately she looked away. "The other man joined us on the prairie." A sudden thought came to her. "I believe he had heard about the reward. They have the wire fixed and they offered a reward for whoever found my father and me. I was not gone, but at Fort Sanders they thought I had been taken with him."

She was still then. Noble had enough to think about. He mulled it over in his mind. "How'd I know I'd get the reward?"

She looked astonished. "Why, of course you would! You've been a gentleman, and I will tell them that! I'd tell them how thoughtful you've been. You saved my life!"

He rinsed out a coffee cup and filled it. She accepted it, although the cup was dirty, and she drank the coffee. It was good, very good. She told him so. He passed her a tin plate with bacon on it and she ate it daintily, carefully. Her hunger was such that she scarcely noticed the plate. Then she drank more coffee and he used the same cup and later the same plate.

She watched him eat, wiping the grease from her fingers on the grass by her side. She looked away, her glance touching on the tree trunks, on the rocks . . . had something moved over there?

73

No. . . .

He was thinking, and she was worried about the direction his thoughts might take. "You're a very good plainsman, aren't you? I noticed the way you studied the country and guided your horse."

"Sure." He wiped his greasy fingers on his pants, then on his shirt. "Good as any full-blood Injun. Been at it all my life. Good in a swamp, too, and woods. I growed up with the Cherokees down yonder."

"No wonder, then. I think they would hire you as a scout for the Army."

He did not care for that. "Not much they wouldn't. I don't like that Army stuff. Like to do as I please. That's one reason I left Parley."

"Parley?"

"Him. The one who has your pa. He tries to run his outfit like we were sodgers. Calls hisself 'Major'. He ain't no more major than me."

"Why don't we ride on to Fort Sanders?" she asked him suddenly. "We could go on. You could find your way, I know you could."

"Course I could. But the hosses is tired," he said.

"We could shift from horse to horse like the Mongols did."

"Who? Who's them?"

"The Mongols. Under their leader, Genghis Khan, they conquered most of Asia and much of eastern Europe. Each man had several horses and they would change from horse to horse without stopping. They drank mare's milk and blood from their own horses."

He stared at her. "You don't say! Fighters?"

"Some of the fiercest. They destroyed hundreds of towns."

"Never run into any Blackfeet, I bet. Them Blackfeet, they're mean! Fighters, too. I lived among 'em. I could live among 'em again, too, an' nobody could touch me, even the Army. I can do anything I want," he bragged, "then go 'mong the Blackfeet an' nobody could touch me." He looked at her, his eyes suddenly malicious. "I could take you 'mong 'em and even your pa couldn't find you. Never know what happened to you."

They were on dangerous ground and she said, "I've heard that Indians won't talk, but don't they like presents? Suppose my father offered them presents?"

He shook his head, but she could see he did not like the thought. "Wouldn't do him no good. He'd have to buy you from me, and if I didn't want to sell, I wouldn't have to. Them Blackfeet squaws, they'd soon make a worker out of you! They're real mean. I druther be held by a bunch of bucks any time, than the squaws."

"My father has many friends among the Indians. He is a good friend of Chief Red Cloud."

"Red Cloud's a Sioux. He wouldn't cut no ice with the Blackfeet, nor the Cherokee neither." Noble got to his feet. "You bed down right there. We'll pull out come midmornin'."

He went to see to the horses and she pulled handfuls of grass to make her bed softer. Her fingers touched a round, fist-sized rock. She took it and placed it where she would be able to put a hand on it. She looked for a short stick she might use as a weapon, but found none. There had been several, but they were in the fire, burning a little.

She sat down, her back against the tree. Through the leaves she could see the sky, the same morning sky she had seen at home in Maryland . . . how long ago, how far away.

Thinking back to her schooldays, her grandmother, her home . . . it was unbelievable that she was here, under these circumstances. But one never knows from any single minute to the next when the sudden change may come. One may drop from peace into horror in an instant.

Realizing this startled her. Life had always been easy. Not that she liked Army camps at first, or that she thought her life easy then, but now she could see how very protected she had been, how surrounded by civilization, by the borders, rims, edges, conventions and rituals of civilization. She realized how little she really knew of the world because of these things that men have

75

made, yet how easily they could all dissolve, destroying even those who most wished for change.

She had been restless with it. She had felt there should be more, not understanding how ill-equipped she actually was to face trouble. She had longed for the wilderness more than once, but when she went into the fringes of it she always prepared a lunch from the things she could buy, and she went provided with the protections her world could give.

Here there was none of that. She was alone with a man who seemed a little less than human, a man who believed he might do anything and escape, scot-free, into the camps of the Blackfeet.

She edged back against the tree, feeling for the stone. It reassured her to have it near. A gun would have been better, but she remembered something her father had said when she commented on the advantage rifles gave the Army. He had said, "Don't forget, my dear, that for a million years before rifles were invented men killed each other with clubs or stones. A thrown rock can kill just as effectively as a fired bullet."

The coolness of the rock felt good in her hand. She replaced it on the ground, suddenly wishing it were larger, a thought that startled her. She had never wished to kill anything, had always said she never would, but suddenly the circumstances were different.

She leaned her head back against the tree and after a moment her weariness became too great and she dozed. Suddenly something moved near her and her eyes flared open. He was standing over her. "Get up!" he said. "I ain't a-goin' to take you back!"

She remained where she was. "You injure me in any way and you'll be hanged for it."

"Hell!" he said. "They'd never find me. Among the Blackfeet—"

Her anger flared. "Don't be a fool!" she said, and she got to her feet, the rock in her hand sheltered by her body. "Only last month the soldiers went into a Blackfoot camp and took out the son of a chief who had killed a man. And they let him go. Times have changed, my friend."

"You lie!" he shouted. "That's a damn lie!"

She had hit him where it hurt, for he must many times have held that out to himself as a refuge, a final escape, a place where he could not be touched. And she had destroyed it.

"It is not a lie." Anger made her bold, and the knowledge that this man, this bully, was trying to frighten her. "It is the truth, and if you lift a hand against me I'll see you turned over to the troopers. They've known me since I was a child. They've made a pet of me. I've been daughter and sister to them all! If you—!"

He stepped back, staring at her. "You think that scares me?" His voice was harsh, but he *was* scared, or bothered at least. "I don't give a damn about them sodgers!" Suddenly his eyes lighted, they looked odd, almost insane. "How'd they know I done anything? I'll do what I want an' when they find you they'll think it was Injuns done it, they'll—"

He stepped toward her then, one hand reaching for her left wrist, the other for her waist.

And she swung the rock.

Barda McClean had been swimming and riding horses since she was a child, spirited horses that needed a strong hand. She swung the rock and she swung it hard. Too late he saw her arm come around; he threw up his arm as the rock hit just back of the temple. He staggered, and she swung it again, quickly, against the side of his head.

He fell, going to his knees. He started to get up, and then collapsed on the ground.

She ran swiftly to the horses. Working faster than she ever had in her life, she saddled and bridled the mare. She drew the cinch tight, then looked over at him.

He was getting up.

Swiftly she turned and ran to the fire, catching up his rifle. Turning, she clucked to the mare, who trotted to her. Barda swung into the saddle.

Pete Noble was on his knees, fumbling for his pistol.

She slapped her heels against the mare's flanks and the animal leaped away. She rode swiftly and hard toward what she believed was the north, and when a mile was behind her she drew up, listening. There was no sound except the distant yammer of a coyote.

Barda looked toward the sun, behind drifting clouds, and got her bearings. She would ride north until she reached the railroad, and then she would ride—

East or west? She might recognize something, but she had no idea what it would be. She thought she must be far west of the little station where the train had stopped, but it was a long, long distance west to the next place, and there were Indians.

After a moment's hesitation, she turned her horse northeast. The search would center around the station, would work out from there, so if she went back there she would be safe, and the nearer she got, the safer she would be.

Far behind her she thought she heard the sound of a shot. She listened, but heard no more. She rode on, walking the mare.

She had no doubt that Pete Noble would follow her, but she doubted he would suspect her of riding toward the northeast. The fear of him was still in her mind, an ugly, unclean thing. Thinking of him, she shuddered.

She had no way of knowing that her fears, so far as he was concerned, were over.

Pete Noble staggered to his feet, dazed and ugly. Blood ran down his face and there was something wrong about his head. He lifted a hand and touched it with delicate fingers. It felt soft, like something had been smashed, and one of his eyes wasn't seeing quite as it should. He leaned against a tree and tried to think.

The girl was gone. He had seen her on a horse with a rifle in her hand. He walked to the fire where he had left his rifle and it was gone. He blinked slowly. There was a gathering pain in his skull. He poured coffee into the cup and gulped it, filled it again and straightened up, and everything seemed to be spinning.

Suddenly his eyes came to a focus and Murray was standing across the fire from him, tough, cold, hawk-faced Murray.

"Parley wants to know where the horses are?"

Noble waved a hand. "Yonder. In the trees. I got some of them."

"And let the girl make a fool of you."

"There was a reward! I—!"

"I saw it, Pete. I saw what you tried to do, and you let a snip of a girl best you. Hell, Pete, Parley was right. You're good for nothing, and you're hurt. I think you've got a skull fracture, Pete, and if I let you stay here and the Army comes up—"

"I'll ride along. I'm all right."

"We can't take a chance on you, Pete. You ran the first time somebody turned a gun on you. I'll take the horses back for you, Pete. I'll tell them you just couldn't make it. I'll explain everything to Parley for you."

"If you'd do that, I'd—"

"I'll tell them how it was, Pete," Murray said, "but we can't take a chance on you naming names or anything. We just can't."

"Then what—?"

"This, Pete. Only this." Murray drew and fired almost in the same instant. Noble saw the hand move and he reached, but the nerveless fingers that grasped the gun butt were already dead fingers.

Murray bent over, took Noble's watch, a few dollars from his pocket, and his pistol. "I'll sell it to some Injun," Murray muttered. "Ought to bring three, four dollars."

He mounted and turned his horses toward the northeast.

"You couldn't do it, Pete," he said aloud, "but I can."

In the early morning light, after a mile or so, he picked up the trail of a walking horse.

79

Chapter Eight

Cris Mayo was circling the rocky hill when he saw another set of tracks, a single horse this time, coming up out of the brush. He hesitated, not liking the idea of two men. Both horses were shod, so it was likely that both were white men. Of course, there was the possibility of an Indian on a stolen horse.

Warily he moved forward. He was fortunate in the horse he rode, for the big beast not only had stamina but was extremely sensitive to the moods of the rider, and seemed to have an awareness of when to be still. Nostrils distended, ears pricked with interest, the gelding walked around the hill.

All was silent. Cris caught a faint smell of smoke, nothing more. Rifle in his hands, he urged the big horse steadily forward, alert for any shot. There were many openings in the brush and he noted them with worry, for he could see that despite alertness he was a sitting duck for a concealed rifleman.

He came suddenly into the camp, and the first thing he saw was Noble's body. The gelding did not like the smell of death, so he tied it to some brush and walked over.

A single bullet . . . right through the heart. Barda had certainly not fired that.

The fat man's pockets were turned inside out, his pistol gone. It was then that Cris paid attention for the first time to the other wound, noting the bloody hair just back of the temple. The man had been struck hard, very hard indeed, before he was killed.

Walking around the camp, Cris found nothing else except a confusion of tracks, and, near a tree, a bloody stone. The sort of thing one could grasp in the hand. That was likely to have been Barda, for a man armed with a gun would not use a rock.

Barda was gone, the horses were gone, the second man was gone.

Cris was learning. Mounting, he made a semicircular sweep on the north side of camp, from which the riders were most likely to emerge. Finding the tracks was no problem. A tight bunch of led horses, heading northeast.

He considered that. Barda was either with this man or he was following her. A few minutes of rapid switching back and forth over the ground showed no other tracks. Cris was, he deduced, but a short time behind them, for the dead man's body had retained some warmth when he touched it.

From a shoulder of the rocky hill he scanned the country. Far off, he thought he glimpsed a tiny plume of dust. He looked to his rifle, then rode down off the hill and put the gelding into a canter.

Riding gives a man a time to think. Where Rep and the colonel had gotten to, he had no idea, but his hunch was that all parties concerned were now riding toward the railroad and the tiny station where it had all begun. The direction was right.

After several miles he slowed his horse, walked into a bottom near a slough, dismounted, and let it drink. When he started on again, he walked, leading the gelding. He was going to come up on them, but there was no need to kill a horse in doing so.

Twice he crossed old trails, both groups of unshod ponies.

Several miles to the east, ten riders were pointing toward the station from the southeast. Justin Parley, Silver Dick Contego and Del Robb led the group. They had recovered ten horses; several had returned to camp, the others they had rounded up near water. Two men were out now scouring the plains for the rest.

"He'll head right back for the railroad," Parley said. "And this time we'll kill him, and when the train comes in, we'll loot it."

The men who rode with him were the toughest of the

lot, and ready for anything. They were men of violence who had known no other way. Their initial hatred was for Sherman, but now McClean was added to the list, and in his pocket they had found what they'd missed when first searching him, a small piece of extremely thin paper on which his orders had come to him.

It was Contego who found the orders and passed them over to Parley. The uniform coat had been left behind when McClean escaped, and Contego had gone through it, discovering the orders.

They were simple and direct. He was "to proceed with utmost speed to Fort Sanders, there to confer on the possible rerouting of the Union Pacific tracks, and on the dispute between Durrant and Dodge." Copies of the order had been sent to Generals Grant, Sherman, Sheridan, and Haney, as well as to Colonels Seymour and McClean, and to several civilians concerned with the development of the railroad.

Parley read, reread, then leaped to his feet. "Dick! This is marvelous! We've alerted them, of course, but they'll never suspect! They'll be sure we are fleeing the country!"

"Aren't we?" Silver Dick asked mildly.

"No! Definitely not! Not now, at least. Dick, do you realize what this means? We can grab the *lot* of them!"

Silver Dick had started his coffee cup to his lips. The movement ceased. "You mean you'd try to capture the whole bag? Grant, Sherman, Sheridan—?"

"Why not? Oh, what a blow to strike for the South! What a blow! Why, man, we'd make history!"

"If we lived," Silver Dick replied. "They'll be surrounded thick with soldiers, Major."

"That's perfect! Let them be surrounded, and the more surrounded they are the less they'll fear. They'd never dream of such a thing! Coming right into the fort, and—"

"Major," Silver Dick suggested, setting his cup down and beginning to comb his hair, "why go into the fort at all? If you really mean to attempt this, there's no need to try the fort. Catch 'em on the outside."

Parley stopped. His eyes were brilliant with excitement and it took a moment for the cool words to penetrate his enthusiasm. "What did you say?"

"They'll undoubtedly go huntin'. All of them are hunters, and I doubt if any one but Dodge has ever hunted buffalo. I may be mistaken, but I'll lay you a hundred that Durrant's planned something of the sort. He knows he's in trouble. He's been buildin' more track than necessary, because the company's making a fat profit on it, and he's going to want to soothe 'em down and win 'em to his side if he can. You can be sure he'll have planned a hunt."

Parley sat down and filled a cup, thinking. Del Robb sat up, his eyes suddenly bright. Robb was a daring man. He had been a sergeant in the Army of the Confederacy, he was a Georgian, and the idea of kidnapping and executing General Sherman had immediately appealed to him. But compared with the development, that plan was nothing, simply nothing at all.

"We'd have to expect a dozen, at least," Parley mused. "The officers, Durrant, probably several of their aides; and there'd be a scout or two, and probably a wagon with food supplies, skinners, and a few helpers trailing behind."

"Yes," Silver Dick commented, "and there's a lot we can do, Major, if you approve. We saw some buffalo a few days ago, part of that herd we stampeded. There's bound to be more nearer to the fort. Send a few men over there, have 'em drift a herd into the breaks along the river. There's feed there; let the buff alone and they'll graze there. And in the breaks we'll have our men."

"How do we know the Yanks would come that way?" Robb objected.

Contego smiled. "We'll just slide a man into the town to alert Barnes and all. They can keep an eye on things, and drop a few words about the buffalo they saw along the river not so far from the fort."

"Good!" Parley was pleased. "That should do it."

"Yeah?" Robb said cynically. "Who goes into Fort Sanders?"

"Murray would be the man if he was here, but you could do it, Del."

Robb chuckled unpleasantly. "I figured you'd lead to that! Why not you?"

"All right," Contego replied, "if the major wants it, I'll be glad to go."

Robb was irritated. He'd conceived the suggestion as one planned by Contego to be rid of him, but now it seemed he had by his doubt given Contego the chance he wanted, to go into the town of Fort Sanders himself, to contact Holly Barnes and the dozen or so men there and . . . "Oh, I'll go!" he protested. "I just didn't want to be saddled with no job just to be got rid of."

"Who'd consider such a thing?" Silver Dick asked, innocently. "I don't care who goes, as long as he stays out of trouble. We need somebody who can listen, understand what he hears, and get word back to us."

"You, Dick," Parley said. "You . . . and Murray, if he gets back. Otherwise I'll pick somebody else. Tillotson, for example."

"He'd be a good man," Contego agreed. Far better, he decided, than Murray, who was a sour, cantankerous and suspicious person with a gun hand as fast and casual as Del Robb's. Contego had more than one idea on his mind and Tillotson would interfere with none of them; Murray might interfere with all.

Silver Dick Contego was a realist. The plot to seize Grant, Sherman and the rest was logical, and apt to succeed by its very unexpectedness. There were catches, however, and he thought he knew what they were.

"We'll have to catch McClean again," he said. "Or at least, keep him from Fort Sanders, where he might recognize us. The girl hasn't seen any of us, I believe."

"She saw me," Robb said, "on the train."

"That's hard luck. But I doubt if she'd remember you," said Contego, "you weren't in that car but half a minute, and there was an almighty to-do goin' on."

So they rode north toward the lonely station, to recapture McClean, and to kill Reppato Pratt, whom somebody had recognized when he effected McClean's escape.

"And there's the other one," Robb said after a while, "that one who cut loose from up on the hill. Whoever he is, I want him."

Across the wide blue sky, only a few clouds drifted now. Upon the prairie the grass stirred with the wind, and here and there were the black dots of buffalo or the gray or amber of antelope. The plains rolled on to the far horizons, mile upon mile on every side. And over the grasslands the horsemen rode, in their several groups.

A lone girl on a mare; and, only a mile or so behind her now, Murray. Further east, the ten renegades led by Parley; and coming up on the trail of the girl, Cris Mayo of County Cork. A lone Irishman on a splendid big horse, an Irishman in a square-topped hat with a rifle he had only begun to use, a six-shooter he had fired but a half-dozen times, and a deep worry about the girl he had been trailing.

Already at the tiny red station, with a signal set to stop the next train, were Reppato Pratt and Colonel McClean, the latter fretting with anxiety over his daughter.

At Fort Sanders, Generals Grant, Sherman and Sheridan were talking over old times, waiting for Dodge, the engineer who was building the railroad, to join them. Waiting too for some word from McClean, a friend to every one of them.

Cris Mayo was hot and tired, sore from much unaccustomed riding, dearly wanting a bath and a meal and a chance to simply rest; and none of these were anywhere in sight.

On his jaws had grown a rusty stubble of beard, his hat was cocked at an angle, his eyes squinted against the glare of the sun. And still far ahead of him showed that tantalizing dustcloud that might be Barda and her tracker . . . or captor.

Quite by accident he came upon a muddy area and following it back into a fold of the hills scarcely three feet deep, he found a trickle of water emerging from between rock layers. He got down from the gelding and drank long. He dipped water into his hat and held it for the gelding to drink, again and again. Then he bathed his face and head, washed his hands and dried them on his shirt.

He sat down for a short rest, his head hanging while the horse tugged at some parched brush that must be more appetizing than it looked.

Back in the saddle, he shoved the rifle into its scabbard and rode forward.

Slowly, slowly, afternoon waned, with the shadows reaching out first from the peaks and shoulders of the hills, then from the few trees and shrubs. He fell into a path made by the wheels of some long-forgotten traveller who had ventured into the area in a covered wagon. They took a general trend eastward, almost parallel to the trail taken by Barda and the other, whoever he was.

The trail vanished and he left his wagon tracks to hunt for it. Suddenly, far ahead among the low blue hills and caught by the last rays of a sun setting behind him, he saw a finger of smoke rise.

It had to be them.

He started to point toward it, and took a sight on a nearby ridge to use if the smoke disappeared, then saw that his wagon trail was swinging that way. He followed it, keeping the smoke, fading now, off to his right.

The hills drew closer. A delightful coolness descended on the plain, the growth was denser, the grass taller. In this place there must be some subirrigation from underground springs in the low hills before him, and in these hills Barda must surely be a prisoner. Unless she had met, thought Cris for the first time, cheering up a little, someone like Rep Pratt.

The big gelding was weary now, and he patted it on the shoulder. "It's a fine horse you are, indeed, and you'll be havin' a good sleep this night if I must walk the rest of the way!"

The hills were low, perhaps no more than seventy or eighty feet above the plain. There were some rocky outcrops, some trees that looked like cedars, and, invisible from the other corner of the hills where Barda and her supposed captor had gone, some cottonwoods.

The wagon trail rounded a low ridge and he found himself facing an old cabin, a shed and a corral, all in the last stages of disrepair. The corral, where animals had once been held, was carpeted with green grass, the soil enriched by the droppings of horses in times long past.

There was a rusty pipe from a spring, a water trough with crystal-clear water, the sides of the trough coated with green moss. He let the big horse drink, then took it to the corral and stripped off the gear. The horse rolled in the grass, then staggered up and began to feed.

Rifle in hand, Cris Mayo walked to the house. The inside was dark, but he struck a match and looked around. A pack rat had been busy here, his deserted nest leaving a nice gathering of fuel. There was a fireplace, an old iron kettle, a sagging bed and a table. The shutters hung loose on leather hinges, and there was no glass, if there ever had been, in the windows.

Chapter Nine

Cris Mayo walked outside. The stars were appearing, and there would be an early moon. He was going to need it.

"You stay here," he told the horse. "I'll be back for you."

Taking up his rifle he walked past the corral to the thin trail he had seen that led up the mountainside. It was worn and packed down by much walking, for whoever had lived in the cabin had found frequent use for the trail. Following it even in semi-darkness was no problem.

Several times he stopped to catch his breath, for he was tired. The rocks became more frequent, the brush taller, with here and there a few trees. He went past the bole of a big old cottonwood, climbed a few steep natural steps in the hillside, and suddenly he was looking down into a small basin, open on one side to the prairie.

A fire threw its light upon the flanks and legs of the horses, on the saddles, and on Barda.

She was sitting near a shrub to which her right hand was tied. Her feet were apparently also bound, although he could not see any ropes. She was seated on a saddle blanket facing the fire where a lean, hatchet-faced man squatted with a frying pan over the fire. The man wore a belt-gun, which Cris could see when the man moved, and his rifle lay on the rock nearby. They were not more than a hundred feet away. In the stillness of the night and the clear air, he could hear the man talking but could not quite make out what he was saying.

Cris crouched down, his weariness forgotten. He was under no false impressions of what could lie ahead. This man was obviously one of the renegades, and he had Barda a prisoner. Without doubt he was also the trigger-man who had killed the fat fellow, killed and robbed him. And that heart-shot indicated that the man was a marksman.

Carefully, Cris studied the hillside before him. Ahead and to his left was a low rock, beyond it a slender bush. If he could manage to get down there. . . .

No rock must rattle, no sound be made. This man was certainly quick and dangerous. Moving from behind the bulge of earth where he had stopped, Cris moved from rock to rock, carefully then through the grass to the bush he had chosen. It was not enough for cover, but he crouched there a moment before going on.

He studied what lay ahead, and there was almost no shelter. Nor could he risk a shot from where he squatted, aside from the fact that he had no desire to shoot a man in cold blood. There were rocks around the fire and a bullet might ricochet . . . he knew little about such things . . . and kill or injure Barda McClean.

He stood up and, choosing his footsteps carefully, started toward them.

The man by the fire rose slowly, put down his frying pan and walked over to Barda. Cris froze in place, his rifle waist-high, watching the man, who stopped behind the girl and said, "Now you just set still, missy, and you won't get hurt."

Then the man lifted his head and at the same time his gun. "All right, sonny," he said, his tone taunting, "you just drop that rifle and walk down to the fire where I can see you. You shoot at me and you're liable to hit your little friend here."

Crispin Mayo hesitated only a moment. He could be shot dead at that range, and he dared not fire back. He dropped the rifle, and, on orders, his six-shooter as well.

"Down to the fire where I can have a look at you, and don't try to be brave or you're a dead man."

Cris walked slowly to the fire, desperately seeking something he might do. Dead he was no good to either himself or Barda, alive there might be a chance. So he must quietly obey.

"Turn around now and face me."

Cris turned. From the corner of his eye he could see Barda, her face deathly white and frightened.

"A mick . . . a damned Irishman! Nobody but an Irishman would dress like that! Well, what d'you know? My name is Murray, friend, and I've some of the blood in me, so maybe I won't kill you."

"The lady's father is worried," Cris said, speaking carefully. "He'll be at the station by now, and you could take her there and nothing will be said."

Murray smiled, not a pleasant smile. "I ain't likely to do that. You see, I killed one man for her, so I'm going to keep her. But I don't want to kill you much. If you want to die, of course, well, that's up to you."

"Don't!" Barda cried out. "Don't you hurt him!"

Murray chuckled. "This is the brave lad who messed up our plans, isn't it? Stampeded our horses . . . I wonder how brave he is?"

"I'm as brave as you, Mister Murray," Cris said. "If you'd be puttin' down that gun I'd be up to showin' you a thing or two." He lifted his left hand. "One hand would do it. One hand is all I'd need to break you in two."

Abruptly, Murray's tone was ugly, the bantering mood was gone. "One hand, huh? How many fingers to a hand, you shanty-Irish bum? How many?"

"Five, I'm thinkin', just five."

"Five! He can count! Do you want to try for four? Put that hand, fingers spread wide, against the log by the fire."

Crispin Mayo was very still. For a moment he could not believe what he heard, but then he knew. The man was not joking. "And if I don't?" he asked.

"Then I'll shoot you right in the belly and let you fall into the fire and toast there while we eat our supper." Murray chuckled sardonically. "Miss McClean can sit comfortable here and watch it."

Cris measured the distance between them. Not a chance. He could have been no further away than this when he killed that fat man back there, and that shot was right through the heart.

90

"Put your hand against that log and spread your fingers. Maybe if you got nerve enough, and can hold steady enough, you won't get hit. I want to show the lady here how I can shoot."

There was no way out that he could see. He squatted down, spreading the fingers of his left hand wide against the side of the old gray log beside the fire. The heat on his hand was intense.

Murray came two steps closer. No more than a dozen feet between them now in the flickering firelight. The bellow of the gun smashed against Cris' eardrums and something stung his fingers. Tiny slivers of wood, for the bullet had struck between his first and second fingers. Murray laughed.

He turned his head slightly and said, "How was that, fair lady? Ever see anybody shoot like that?"

His eyes returned. "All right now, sonny. Five fingers, you said? Would you like to die? Or live with just a thumb on that hand? You've got a choice, boy."

Cris said, "I'd like to live."

Murray laughed. "Now you'll see, honey, what you can expect if you don't do as you're told . . . see?" The gun bellowed, and Cris felt a sharp sting. He stared. The end of his little finger was gone!

He started to move, seeing blood well from it. "Hold it there, boy!" snapped Murray. "You can try for three now! But you make one move, even a tremble, and you get it right through the skull."

Murray eared back the hammer and in that instant Cris dropped his wounded hand into the hot coals and swept a great handful of flame and sparks at Murray. One quick thrust and fling, and the air was filled with glowing coals and leaping fire.

Murray sprang back, yelling, startled; as the embers struck his hand, he dropped the gun.

He stooped, grabbing for it, and Cris Mayo was over the fire and at him. His knee smashed into Murray's brow, knocking him sprawling on his back. Cris rushed in but churning feet and flashing spurs drove him back. Murray came off the ground, lips curled in a snarl as he dove at Cris.

91

All pain was forgotten now. This was a type of fighting he understood, and Cris smashed a left into the charging face and felt Murray's nose crunch under his fist. The gunman flailed at him with frantic fists, but Cris stepped in, slipped a wild left and hooked a wicked right into the other man's ribs. Murray grunted, grabbed at Cris and stabbed a thumb at his eyes. Cris turned his head . . . this was old stuff, he'd learned that trick when he was fourteen, at Rosscarbery . . . and smashed another blow to the ribs and another to the ear.

Murray staggered and almost fell, but Cris picked him up with his left and struck him four times in the face, then in the belly. Murray tried to knee him in the crotch but Cris Mayo knew what to do about that, too. He lifted his own knee, turning it sidewise and the effort failed.

He shoved Murray off and struck him again in the belly, then again, and then he stopped and spread his legs and began throwing them from the hips, brutal, battering punches that knocked Murray around as if he was but a leaf in the wind.

Murray went down to stay, and Cris walked over and picked up the fallen man's gun. He walked back to Murray and turned him over with one boot. There was a second pistol—Pete Noble's—in his belt, which Cris took also. Murray made no effort to move, so Cris walked to Barda, picked up a knife from beside the fire, and cut her free. "Your finger!" she gasped. "Your poor finger!"

She got to her feet, staggering from being so long tied up. He took Murray's gun in his right hand and held out the left to her. "Bind it up, if you can. We've got to get out of here."

"But we can't leave now! You're hurt!" She began to bandage the finger with a couple of dainty handkerchiefs that were all but inadequate for the job. Yet the hot coals had partially cauterized the wound, even in the fraction of a second of their contact with it.

"Somebody may have heard those shots, and maybe

they are his friends and maybe they'll be coming this way," said Cris.

He went to the horses, saddled her mare and gathered the guns, his and Murray's. He helped her onto the mare and saw Murray slowly moving as though to rise. "If you're smart," he said quietly, "you'll stay down. Though you're a bloody and cruel man, I'd not be for beatin' you further unless you ask for it. But if you cross my path again, I'll not let up a second time. If I see you, I'll come for you, fist or gun or club, as to your liking, and to a finish."

He swung up on one of the horses bareback and walked them all away up the hill, with Barda taking the trail beside him. His finger hurt abominably. On the far side of the hill he dismounted, saddled the best looking of the captured horses, and scattered the others with shouts and slaps; then, leading the colonel's horse, they started away.

"What will he do there?" she asked.

"He's got water nearby, and he's got whatever grub he had. When he's able to move, he'll get out. Maybe his friends will find him, and if they do not, he will find his way. He's a mean man and a tough one."

Crispin Mayo looked up at the stars, then swung the horses a bit to the west of north. They rode steadily. "We'll be goin' to the station now," he said. "I'm thinkin' there will be trains, and your father may be there, and this will soon be a bad dream in your mind and no more."

"You are a brave man, Crispin Mayo, a very brave man."

"I'd not claim that. I was afraid yonder. I knew the man had a cruelty in him that would not be satisfied with missing me, nor with a finger even. He'd have shot me to pieces, then killed me."

He had taken the time to hold his burned hand in cold water after the fight, while saddling the colonel's horse when he was beside the trough, but it hurt. Yet his hand had been in the coals only a moment, a swift dash of the arm that had given little time for burning or anything else, and still its tip had been slightly cauterized. That surprised him.

Far on the horizon, low down, he saw a red star. And then he was sure. It was no star at all, but the station, and there was a red lantern burning there. They had not been far from it at all.

He slowly drew closer, looking to the welcoming light as to that of his own home, and eager to be there. Now it would be only minutes. . . .

They had dipped down into a hollow and were coming out of it when he heard the galloping of a party of horsemen. Suddenly there was a shot and the welcoming light was gone and he heard wild rebel yells and shots, and he swung down from the horse. "Hold them!" he said. And dropping to one knee, he leveled at the dark mass where the riders were and opened fire with his rifle, two quick shots, then a dash off to the left, and another shot. Back to the right and another, trying to make them believe they faced several riflemen.

Bullets replied, most of them from pistols and too far off, and then they wheeled their horses and rode off, not wishing to come up against riflemen on the ground and hence in a better firing position.

Keeping on the side of the low embankment on which the station stood, the man and the woman walked forward. Fifty feet off, Cris stopped and called out in a low voice. "Is it you then, Reppato?"

"Sure it is! Come on in!"

They walked in, leading their horses, and Rep came to the door, a gun in his hand, then Colonel McClean. Barda ran to him and for a moment they clung together, each demanding to know if the other was all right.

"Crispin took care of me, father. I am all right, but he's got a burned hand and a finger shot off."

"I taken care o' you, too," Reppato said grumpily, "for awhile."

"Of course you did! And I am grateful for it."

"Was that you shooting?" McClean asked.

"It was. I saw them against the sky, and knew them for what they were; then they opened fire and I had them flanked."

94

"Good man! I doubt if they'll try again tonight, and there will be a train with soldiers on it at daybreak. The train will take us through to Fort Sanders."

Reppato Pratt walked to the corner of the room where Crispin was already settling down with an extra blanket from the bedroom. "You lost a finger?"

"From the first joint only. He was showing his marksmanship to her. I knew he'd put one in my belly soon, or break a knee first, or something, so I swept coals in his face and went after him. His name was Murray."

"*Murray!*" Rep grasped his shoulder. "Did you kill him? If not, you better go back an' do it."

"I did not. But he will remember me. I broke his nose over his face and I'm thinking he has some staved-in ribs. I gave him a fearful beating and I'm thinkin' he will not wish to come for me again."

They slept then, while the colonel and Rep kept watch, and in the clear, cold hour before the dawn they heard a far-off sound, a sound they all wished to hear . . . a train whistle, winding lonesomely against the hills, and like it there is no other sound.

Crispin Mayo came to his feet, then sat again and drew on his brogans. He was dog-tired and his hand hurt in every bit of it, but soon he'd be on the train again. It would be a few days before he could handle a pick or a hammer, but his hand would heal.

The train whistled again and Rep struck a light in one of the lanterns. He waved it and the churning wheels of the train ground to a stop.

They stood on the small platform, and the conductor stepped down. It was Sam Calkins. "You?" he said to Cris. "I thought you'd run out on our fight."

"I left one man last night with a broken nose and ribs, and I can leave another. Get a ramp down and load the horses, man, the colonel cannot wait."

Calkins started to reply but McClean interrupted. "Do as he says, and quickly."

Seated in the train again, Crispin Mayo leaned his head against the back of the seat and put his hat over his eyes. "Do not disturb me until we're there," he said to Rep, and went to sleep.

The whistle whined lonesomely against the dying night, and the steam engine chugged away, dragging its many-eyed dragon behind.

Far out upon the prairie, Justin Parley watched it go. "There will be another day," he said, "and soon."

Chapter Ten

Fort Sanders was a frontier settlement, formerly known as Fort John Buford, established to protect the tie-cutters and grading crews working west of Cheyenne. A few squatters had appeared before the railroad, but by the time the rails reached the site there were several hundred buildings, shacks and cabins of logs, sod, canvas, railroad ties and old wagon boxes, near the fort, and within hours Laramie, as it now called itself, was a booming town.

Crispin Mayo and Reppato Pratt stood on the narrow platform at what passed for the station. "Seen towns like this before," Rep said; "if'n you got money you can git yourself trouble. Without it you cain't git the time o' day."

Cris fingered his few coins, not enough to take him anywhere. "We must make some money, then. This isn't a town to be hard-up in."

"How you gonna do that? Rob somebody?"

"That conductor now . . . Sam Calkins? He fancies himself. I wonder if he's known here?"

"He's won three fights, London Prize Ring rules, at end-of-track towns. I seen one o' them, an' he's good. He's a bruiser."

"That's it, then." Cris was looking at a sign over a walled tent. It said, BRENNAN'S BELLE OF THE WEST—SALOON & GAMBLING.

Cris strolled down the street and went in. A dozen games were going, the bar was crowded, girls were circulating among the tables. There was a board floor under their feet and board siding to the tent. He pushed his way through the crowd, Pratt following, protesting.

A man leaned on the back bar. His hair was slicked down upon his large head, his mustache was walrus in style, but neatly trimmed. His face was florid, and looked hard as polished oak. He was a big man and a gold chain with an elk's tooth hung across his chest.

"Brennan?"

Cold eyes turned upon Crispin.

"I am."

"And I am Crispin Mayo, from County Cork."

Brennan took the cigar from his mouth. "I am from Donegal, and we're full up. I need no help. Seven of any ten men on the track are Irish, so don't play on that. I've no free drinks, no free lunch, and no money to give or lend."

"I said I am Crispin Mayo from County Cork, and I don't give a damn for your money, your beer, your food, or your manners. I've known folk from Donegal before this, and they were gentlemen, which you obviously are not."

Brennan dusted the ash from his cigar. "If I had the time I'd throw you out," he said, "but I'm going to be kind enough to let you walk out. If you don't do it soon, under your own steam, I'll have it done for you."

"It's a poor man who'll hire his fightin' done for him," Cris said coolly, "but I'd be pleased to whip the lot of what you have here except that I've come on business. Do you know Sam Calkins?"

"I know him."

"He does not like me. Nor does he like the Irish."

"So?"

"He has spoken of fighting me when the mood is on him, and I've a thought the mood would come if there was a purse and maybe a side bet."

"You wish that I'd bet on him to whip you? I would. Sam is a good fighter, and I've never seen you before."

"No man who runs a gambling house would be the fool you'd have to be to bet against a man you did not know. I want to fight him."

"Why?"

"I need the money. I want a purse raised. Two hundred dollars."

Brennan was amused. "So you take a beating and collect part of the purse?"

"I want to fight winner-take-all."

Brennan put his cigar down on the edge of the bar. There was a row of burns where other cigars had been left. "You would be the fool he takes you for, then. Sam Calkins is no whiskey-soaked loudmouth. I do not like him, but he is a first-class fighting man. No country boy from Ireland is going to whip him."

"Winner-take-all, I said. You are from Donegal. Have you heard of Bully Crogan?"

"I have."

"Three summers ago I threw him three straight falls at the fair in Mallow."

Brennan was no longer contemptuous, but he was a cautious man. "Crogan was a strong man and a good wrestler," he said, a grudging respect in his tone now. "But he was not a boxer. This is not wrestling."

"Nor am I a wrestler by any manner of preference. I wrestled because that was what Crogan did."

Brennan glanced at Cris' knuckles. "It seems to me you've been busy already."

Cris shrugged. "It was not that kind of fight. There was a man named Murray, one of Parley's outfit, and he had Barda McClean, the colonel's daughter. It was a bad thing he had done, and I wished to take the girl to her father. Murray objected."

"I expect he would." Brennan watched Cris with cold, curious attention. "You took her from Murray?"

"I did that."

"Be careful, then. Murray is a vengeful man and he'll be coming for you with a gun."

"Not for a few days, I'm thinkin'. He'll have trouble breathing with a broken nose and caved-in ribs."

Brennan took up his cigar. "Do you think you can beat Calkins?"

"I do."

"Have you ever seen him fight?"

"I have not. It is a feeling I have. I can beat him."

"All right, then. I will arrange it, but if you welsh on me I'll have you killed."

Cris looked into the cold eyes and had no doubt of it. "I'll not welsh, and I'll beat him."

He started to turn away, but Brennan's voice stopped him. "You'll need eating money." He placed a twenty-dollar gold piece on the counter, then his eyes slanted to Reppato Pratt. "I know you, Pratt. Are you a friend of his?"

"You could say that, I reckon. Cris is all right."

"Then stand by him and keep your gun handy. Calkins has some rough friends who'll back him in a fight. I'll arrange it for the day after tomorrow, when Calkins is in town from his run."

They walked away. "We will eat now," Cris said, "and then we will relax a bit."

"Do you know what you let yourself in for?" Pratt asked, drily. "Sam Calkins is a pure terror with his fists, and he got no use for you. He'll be out to tear you apart."

"He can try."

Pratt glanced at him. "Maybe you are good," he said. "I'd ruther you was. Calkins needs a whuppin'; you give it to him an' you'll have friends about. But I dread the man's fists. I can use a gun or an Arkansas toothpick, but fists ain't for me."

There was a tent with a sign MEALS across the front, and they went in. A long plank table stretched down the center of the tent, benches lined either side. It was past the hour, but a dozen men were scattered along the table eating from high-piled platters of buffalo and venison steaks, bowls of beans, and a big pot of coffee.

They paid twenty-five cents to a burly man with immense forearms and rolled-up sleeves, and they loaded their plates. "This here's not much of a genteel town. Cock-fightin's the thing, dog-fightin', too. Onct they matched a bear an' a bull . . . bear won. They'll be wantin' a *fight,* not no fancy stuff, and Sam Calkins knows it. You know any dirty fightin'?" Rep inquired doubtfully.

100

"I do."

"You'll be needin' it, then. Sam knows ever' trick there be."

Maybe he did and maybe he didn't, but Irish farmers and fishermen were rough men, and the fighting at county fairs had been nothing like a pink tea party. And of course, when it came to really dirty fighting, he'd learned that along the waterfronts and aboard the sailing ship.

"What about your hand?"

Cris glanced at it. He'd have to tape that little finger. Bandage it good. When he had started off with a fight in mind he had forgotten that finger, but they were broke and he knew no other way of getting money quickly. Now for the first time he considered the finger. The bleeding had been stopped long since, and he thought maybe the finger was in good enough shape. And there were two more days for it to heal.

Brennan was not interested only in a fight. He was a betting man and if his protege could beat Calkins . . . over the bar he was giving it thought. He liked the look of Cris Mayo. A tough young Irishman strong enough to throw Bully Crogan might whip Calkins. Brennan remembered Crogan well, a rough man, powerful, brutal and sadistic. He would have liked fighting a clean-cut youngster like Mayo, would have enjoyed beating him down.

He scowled suddenly. Suppose it was a put-up job? Mayo admitted he had met Calkins, had come in on Calkins' train . . . suppose they had conspired to take his money?

He liked the look of Mayo, but who was altogether honest? He glanced around the room and recognized a tall young cavalryman, a man who he was quite sure had been one of the guard for Colonel McClean.

"You!" he called. "Come here a minute!" The young man got up from his table and walked over, beer in hand. "Do you want a drink? A better drink than that?"

101

"I'm satisfied. What's on your mind?"

"Were you with that train? The one that picked up McClean and his daughter?"

"Sure was. I was on the train when he was taken, too, and they'd put me up at the front and there was no time to do anything. We heard nothing, saw nothing until there was no proper signal at the station, and then we stopped and found the colonel was taken. It was a nervy thing."

"What about this Mayo fellow? What did he have to do with it?"

Briefly, the young cavalryman explained, then added, "He's a tough one. He faced right up to Calkins, who didn't like it one bit."

"They are going to fight."

"Fight?" It dawned on the boy suddenly. "You mean in the ring? I want to see that!"

"How did he look to you? Mayo, I mean."

The calvaryman considered that. "He's well set-up. I'd say he is heavier than he looks. Wider shoulders than most, a slim waist, and he's strong. He put down that ramp all by himself when he took the horses off. It usually takes four men, though two very strong ones might do it."

Brennan took the empty beer glass and slid it down the bar. "Fill it up!" he said, and then casually, "He and Calkins talk much?"

The calvaryman laughed. "Not so you could notice it. Sam tried to run over him and he got just nowhere." He looked up quickly. "If you're thinking this might be arranged, forget it. I was there. Nothing tricky about it, and I'll bet Mayo is hell on wheels in any kind of a fight."

"Thanks," Brennan said. "And have another beer."

"Two's plenty. Mr. Brennan, I want to see that fight. I want very much to see it. I am Tom Halloran."

Brennan was startled. "*You?* Halloran, the foot racer?"

"I was, until I joined the Army. Unfortunately, I may not be able to come. I'm one of the escort for the generals. They're going on a buffalo hunt."

Brennan brushed out his cigar. He was thinking rapidly. He knew all about Halloran: Irish blood, of good family, a college man. He was a foot racer who had begun to run in contests in the East at a time when foot racing was a focal point for gamblers. More money was wagered on foot racing than on fighting, and in some areas, more than on horse racing. Many a sprinter was drifting about the country, passing himself off as some country bumpkin until he could find men to bet against him.

Halloran had run a number of times . . . then there had been a shooting. He remembered that. "You're a good man," Brennan said quietly, "and Mayo will need such a man in his corner, one who understands physical conditioning."

"I've worked behind a number of fighters," Halloran said, "but it will depend on two things: the possibility of my being free from duty, and the certainty that you want Mayo to win. I'll have no part of a fix."

"That's why I want you," Brennan said quietly. "How many here know who you are?"

The trooper chuckled. "I am Trooper Halloran, that's all."

"Keep it so," Brennan said.

As Halloran left, Brennan lit another cigar and leaned his forearms on the bar. Rolling the cigar in his teeth, he considered the situation. Sam Calkins had numerous backers who were close friends of Sam's and believed him unbeatable. Brennan, who knew most things happening along the right-of-way of the Union Pacific, frowned thoughtfully. Sam Calkins had curious associates, but for a man who was a pugilist as well as a railroader, that was not surprising. Having told himself that, he took the cigar from his mouth, regarded it with sudden distaste that had nothing to do with the cigar, and placed it on the bar's edge.

Owen Brennan had come to America as a laborer, had given himself a modest education through reading, beginning with a day-to-day study of the newspapers in order to acquaint himself with current beliefs, opinions, and affairs. He saved cuttings from the papers and soon

103

had a file on politicians, sports figures, and military men, as well as a scattering of those in business.

His purpose was simple. He wished to know what was going on and who was making it go, in order to plan his own affairs. Soon he had won a place as a policeman in New York and followed that as a contractor in road building. Not long thereafter he owned a dozen teams and fresnos, those two-handled scoops for the moving of earth that were drawn by horses.

The building of the Union Pacific enabled him to get some right-of-way contracts as well as a chance to do some freighting. The saloon had been an afterthought, but a profitable one that moved westward with the tracks, and besides the selling of much drink it provided a convenient listening post.

Tom Halloran was to be one of the escort for the generals' buffalo hunt. Well, Brennan knew the lad's first sergeant. He could get him out of that.

Chapter Eleven

Cris Mayo finished his meal and refilled his cup. Reppato Pratt sat beside him, lean, tough and watchful. "I don't like it," he muttered after awhile.

Cris, busy with his own thoughts, asked, "What do you not like?"

"Justin Parley an' them. They'd ruther die than quit. They're a murderous lot, an' they want Gen'l Sherman's scalp so bad they can taste it. Far's that goes, they'd like to kill the whole passel o' them high officers."

"Parley missed the chance. They are all here now, at Fort Sanders, with troops gathered about like bees on a hive."

"I know. But it is a worrisome thing, an' I don't believe that lot'll give up so easy. I lived among 'em, an' the most is a tough, vicious lot. I never could figure what Silver Dick was after. He's the smartest one, maybe smarter than Parley. Del Robb, he's been huntin' trouble since he was a least youngster. These folks'd be renegades in their own land, stirrin' trouble there if not here, and most of them were druv out o' wherever 'tis they come from. Until you've seen 'em in action you've no idea how mean folks can git."

"They'll be far from here," Cris said, "they'll be afraid of the cavalry."

"Not much, they won't. They'll fight any small bunch, and they'll stay shy of the patrols big enough to fight them even or better. And the Army has to think of Injuns, too."

Halloran came in and sat down across the table from them. "I just left Brennan," he told them. "He wants

105

me to work in your corner, Mayo. You may recall me from the train. I'm Halloran."

"Howdy," Pratt said. "Don't Brennan reckon I'm good enough?"

"Yes, but he wants you to be around with a gun handy. I have some experience at this sort of thing. Handling athletes, I mean." He looked at Cris. "What kind of shape are you in? Can you go a long fight?"

"I can." He put out his unbandaged left hand. The finger had scabbed over. "Murray shot that off. It might start to bleed. Stop it if you can, when it does."

Startled, Halloran stared. "You'd go into a fight with *that?*"

"I would." Cris glanced at the hand and said, "A man has so much to put up with in his life. I came here to make a fortune and I won't do it sitting about crying because I got scratched.

"I came into this town without money, and I must live. Rep here is in the same boat. I figured with the two hundred dollars I'd win, we'd have enough to tide us over until there is a way to a better living."

"Don't take Sam Calkins lightly. He is heavier than you, very strong. He's a tough, boring-in fighter who's won nine or ten fights against some of the best bare-knuckle battlers around. I believe he will try to wear you down. Very few men can fight more than two or three minutes without running out of steam. If he can do that he'll have you helpless."

"He cannot. I will last as long as any man."

"He tries to work in close. He likes the uppercut. Do you know the blow?"

"I know it."

Halloran was not satisfied. Mayo seemed confident, which was good, but it might be the confidence of ignorance. To a man who has never boxed or fought with a skilled professional, it is easy to believe that only strength and aggressiveness are important. A professional is just as skillful at his trade as is a master cabinetmaker. The beginner can no more do one job as well as the master than he can do the other.

There is nothing fancy about the professional boxer.

He wastes no motions, his every move is timed, his distances are judged, the knowledge of what you can do is in his mind, and he knows that when a punch has been thrown certain portions of the head or body are exposed. He knows how to feint another fighter into exposing the areas where he wishes his blows to land, and he knows how to avoid blows by a hair, moving no more than is necessary. He knows how to work in close so that when a blow is thrown he remains within punching distance.

He knows that the feet should be placed in a certain way for the maximum punching power, and that certain combinations of punches can be thrown to take advantage of his opponents' efforts, and that if the punches are thrown in sequence the openings will be there when the fists arrive.

Halloran had boxed a lot. He also had seen many fights. He had seen bruisers demolished by smaller men who knew what they were about. Sam Calkins knew much of this, how much he did not know. Halloran had been about with some of the great ones, like Jem Mace. The English gypsy was one of the cleverest fighters of his time, who had worked out many of the most advanced tactics in boxing. Yet a boxer must have good competition, for he will not improve beyond the talent required to win over the opponent he faces. The better the competition, the better the fighter; and Halloran knew nothing of the sort of boxing Mayo had done. Had he really faced good men? Or just the common run of country boys with whom he had brawled for the sport of it?

"I'll be in your corner if I can," he said. "Duty may prevent it. I don't know yet."

When he had gone they finished their coffee and walked outside. Down the street was another tent with the sign BEDS. Pratt shook his head when Cris pointed it out. "There's a hotel here, and you'll need rest, not drunks staggerin' in at all hours an' card games a-goin', Cost a mite more, but worth it."

They found a room, paid fifty cents for it, and borrowing a whisk broom he saw at the desk, Cris carefully brushed his clothes and his hat. Then he wiped off his brogans. They were scarred and shabby, but still intact. He washed his striped shirt out and hung it to dry.

"Didn't you say you had a carpetbag on that first train?"

"I did."

"Gimme a description and a note and I'll hunt 'er up for you. Meanwhile, you better get some rest." He glanced at the wet shirt. "You're not goin' anywheres for a while."

When Rep had left, Cris stretched out on the bed in his underwear. He clasped his hands behind his head and thought.

The fight with Sam Calkins had been a logical development. If he defeated Calkins he would have two hundred dollars and he could go on to the west, maybe to California where the McCleans were headed. Brennan might advise him on that. He had no desire to continue fighting, and no real wish to work on the railroad. What he wanted was what he had always wanted, land of his own and a chance to raise the kind of horses he had handled in Ireland.

He had worked as a fisherman, a seaman, and a farm hand. He had cut peat, made hay, and worked with a pick and shovel, a saw and hammer, and as much as he liked the using of tools he longed for a chance to do something more. Land was for the taking, and that would be the first thing.

He thought of Maire. Was she married by now? Wed to that spalpeen they had planned for her? He'd like to go back and show them. He'd like to go back, owning land and cattle and horses and a dozen new suits, and strut around and show them what Crispin Mayo could do.

Much as he wished for it, he knew that it was childish. That he had first to make a place for himself here. Calkins, by his bullying tactics, had opened a door for the chance to make money quicker. His thoughts strayed to Barda, but she was an American colonel's daughter and would have no use for a penniless immigrant Irishman. Why, there were places in the States where an Irishman was not even permitted to go!

Where there were signs advising *No Irish Need Apply!*

He got up, did fifty squats, as many push-ups and sit-ups. He had been doing them for years, morning and evening, unless he was too tired from the work. They were something his uncle had started him on, years before.

He dozed and slept. Suddenly he awakened, hearing a low mutter of voices that at first he could not place. The room was shadowed and still, the evening well along. The voices came through the thin wall.

". . . Calkins'll beat him. He ain't seen any of us, anyway. Only Murray."

"Murray's red-eyed fightin' mad. Figures to kill the mick, but Parley don't want no trouble. Not until after. If he can keep Murray tied down till then he'll be lucky. I never seen a man so mad."

"That mick damn near killed him. Nose an' three ribs, four, five teeth."

"Murray ain't Calkins. You'll see. Ol' Sam will beat him to the ground. I seen him work a time or two."

Their voices dwindled and a door closed. Cris Mayo lay quiet, thinking. Some of the Parley gang were in town. Why? Of course, they'd like to come into town to blow off steam just like anybody else. But what did that mean, "not until after"? After what?

Was something being planned? Or did they just mean that Murray was not to be allowed to have his chance until after the fight? That must be it.

He dozed off, slept solidly again. When he awakened it was completely dark and Pratt was still not back, but there was his carpetbag, just inside the door. Pratt must have returned, found him asleep and gone away again.

He got up and went to the bag. So far as he could see nothing had been taken from it. He pulled on a fresh shirt, folded the one that was now dry and put it away. His finger was sore and kept getting in the way. At every moment he was bumping it.

He got out his six-shooter, emptied it, then buckling on the gunbelt he began practicing with the gun. He had heard of the fast draw but had never attempted it. His hand was awkward at first, but he practiced simply

109

getting a good grip and bringing the gun into position. He was naturally well-coordinated and had worked with his hands all his life, so the movements came easy, before long.

For an hour he worked with the gun, and liked the feel of it. He made no effort to be fast, and believed he was getting the hang of it; at least, of how he thought it should work.

He had no desire to go out on the streets so he sat down, picked up a newspaper from St. Louis that he had found lying in the room, and read through it. There was a little about the railroad, a few references to the fur trade, and much news about people of whom he had never heard.

At Fort Sanders, Colonel McClean was seated at a table with General Haney, the railroad engineer Dodge, and one or two other officers. "By the way, McClean, that young fellow who lent you a hand is a prizefighter."

"Mayo?" McLean was surprised. "I had no idea."

"He's matched with Sam Calkins. The day after tomorrow, in a fight to the finish, London Prize Ring rules."

"I am surprised," McClean said. "In the few minutes I talked with him after we were safe, he seemed quite a decent lad."

"He could be. I've known a number of boxers who were far from the thugs they've been painted, even though the bare-knuckle fighter does not have the associations we would expect from a gentleman.

"Anyway, from what I hear, it started with an altercation about the time they seized you. It seems that Calkins made some unpleasant remarks about the Irish, and your boy is from County Cork."

"I'd like to see it," Dodge said. "I have never liked Calkins. He's a surly brute at best."

"He'll kill the boy," someone said.

"My daughter was quite impressed with him, both his conduct and his strength," McClean commented, "so I am not sure of that. Barda has been around Army camps so long that she's a pretty good judge of men."

Colonel Seymour entered. "Gentlemen, it is settled. We have a hunt arranged. Some buffalo have been sighted over along the river; several hundred of them, in fact. We have a competent guide, a chap named Holly Barnes. He himself saw the beasts. There will be ten in the party, and we should have excellent hunting."

"There's no chance until after our meeting, Seymour. The generals wish you to present your side of the argument, or Durrant's side, rather. Then we'll hear Dodge. So three days from now?"

Seymour frowned. "The buffalo may have moved on. I can promise nothing."

"If there is to be a hunt it must be then," General Haney said firmly, "it cannot be before."

Seymour hesitated. The hunt, which he hoped would be successful, was to get them in the mood for a favorable decision, but he dared not push it against Haney's last statement. "Well, whatever you say, sir. I just hope the beasts don't drift out of the area."

"If they do, Seymour, we will just have to postpone the pleasure, will we not? We did not come west to hunt."

Seymour flushed. After all, this was Durrant's problem, not his. He was prepared to replace Dodge as engineer on the right-of-way if so directed, but it was Durrant who was at war with Dodge, not himself. He had always respected Dodge, who was a highly competent engineer, yet Durrant had considerable influence in many areas and he was a good man to know.

"There's going to be a prizefight," he said, not aware that they knew; "we can go to that. Brennan is backing a man named Mayo, one of the tracklayers, against Sam Calkins, a conductor."

"I am going, McClean," Haney said. "Will you join me?"

"Of course. And I hope Mayo wins. I owe him a great deal."

Barda McClean heard the news from the woman who brought her supper. Crispin Mayo was going to fight! Odd, he had never mentioned being a fighter. (Barda

111

had not overheard his conversation with Rep on that subject.) He had talked a little of Ireland, but nothing of what he did beyond that he was recently over, and had expected to be laying track for the U.P. by now. What had changed his mind?

She combed her hair for an unusually long time that night, thinking about Cris. When her father came in she went to him. "Papa, we should do something for Crispin Mayo. He was so brave, and so quick to help, and he saved my life and helped to save yours. We've never even thanked him properly."

"What would you suggest?"

"First, we might ask him to dinner. Then we could find out what he intends to do. Maybe we could help him."

"We might," he admitted. "But the fellow is a prize-fighter, Barda. There may come a time when that will not be held against a man, but most of them are toughs, associated with gamblers and all manner of low people."

"But he seemed such a gentleman!"

"Many men *seem* so. I do not wish to be unfair, but he is a stranger. If I alone were involved, it would be different; but I have a young, impressionable daughter."

She laughed. "Not so impressionable, papa! And remember! I was alone with him, night and day, while we looked for you. He's not a stranger to me. He was always a gentleman, thoughtful and kind, and very brave."

"By the way," he said suddenly, "we've been invited on a buffalo hunt. General Grant said I was to bring you if you wished to come."

"Of course. I'd love to. I've never even seen one of the beasts up close."

Chapter Twelve

Morning, the day of the fight, dawned with a clear sky. Cris rolled out of the bed in which he had spent two long nights recouping his strength; he stretched, dressed, and went outside into the crisp clear air. It was very early and no one was about.

He walked along the single street, his footsteps echoing hollowly against the walls. The street was muddy from the last raining, the holes still contained water but the mud was hardening.

Brennan's place was closed, and nothing else seemed to have opened. He felt good. "And I'd better!" he told himself. For he was under no illusions. Confident as he was, he knew he had never met a fighting man of Sam Calkins' experience, nor was there any certain way to judge his ability, for they had fought no one in common. That the man was good, he was sure.

He was also sure that today he faced his big chance. He had won a few friends here, but he had no money, and well enough he knew that without money a man could do nothing. The fight was his first and best chance; besides, he did not like Calkins.

If the weather held, the generals would have a fine day for their hunt tomorrow, too. He envied them none at all. The only hunting he had ever done was for meat for his own table . . . well, to be honest, it had been partly for the sport of tricking the gamekeepers. He thought of the coming fight. He must pace himself wisely. Calkins was experienced, so Calkins would try to make him do most of the work in the early rounds. Cris must save himself, move not too much, and be careful not to be caught flat-footed.

He paused by the corner of a building, looking at a horse across the street at the hitching rail. It was a compact bay with a black mane and tail, and it bore a brand that he had seen before. Cris knew nothing about reading brands, only that he had seen this one by clear moonlight and it had belonged to one of the horses he had helped drive away from Justin Parley's camp.

What was it doing here? One of Parley's men still in town? This was certainly the horse he remembered. It was tied not far from Brennan's.

He hung around for several minutes, but nobody came near the horse, so he walked back to the hotel and stretched out on the bed. It was not long before there was a knock at the door and he opened it to Reppato Pratt and Trooper Halloran.

"How do you feel?" they asked in unison.

"Fine," he said. "I walked out and stretched my legs. Are you ready to eat?"

Halloran had eaten at the fort, but they walked together to the tent. The big cook came out and slammed down several trays on the table. He glanced sharply at Cris. "You the one who's to fight Calkins?"

"I am."

"Watch his left. He's good with it, and he hits almighty hard."

"You've seen him fight?"

"*Seen* him? I done fit him! He whupped me, whupped me good. He's mean, no two ways about it. You'll know, this time tomorrow. An' watch him for gougin'. He'll do it. He'll have both your eyes out if you ain't careful."

They ate in silence. Cris Mayo had forgotten about the bay horse and Justin Parley. Back at the hotel time seemed to hold still. Cris paced the floor restlessly, irritably.

About half an hour before fight time, Brennan came around. He looked sharply at Cris. "You're ready, then?"

"I am."

"Come along, I've a carriage outside."

"It's only a few hundred yards. I can—"

"Shut up and get in." In the carriage, which was an old stagecoach, Cris leaned back against the hard cushion, Owen Brennan opposite him. "There's a lot of money bet on this," the saloon keeper said. "I've got three thousand on you myself."

Cris blinked. "Three thousand? *Dollars?*"

"That's right, and there's plenty more been bet. Colonel McClean has bet five hundred." Brennan smiled. "The odds are three to one. I am hoping to get down another thousand at four or five to one before time is called."

Halloran had brought Cris a suit of blue tights of waist length and a pair of good, flat-soled leather shoes of light construction, such as fighters wore. He went into the walled tent saloon and put them on.

A ring had been set up in an open space behind Brennan's *Belle of the West,* and seats had been tiered against the corral with the highest row along the top rail of the corral itself.

A crowd had already gathered, and on a balcony over the back awning of the saloon a row of chairs had been placed. Two officers in blue already sat there, giving them the best view of all.

The crowd was made up of railroad workers, town toughs, soldiers, gamblers, a few women of the louder sort, and a general gathering of townsmen, freighters and the like. Suddenly Colonel McClean appeared on the balcony.

"Gentlemen? *Gentlemen!*" The crowd turned to look. "I have instructed these men," he indicated two soldiers on either side of the balcony, both armed with rifles, "to shoot anyone who attempts to tear down the ring or lay hands on either of the fighters. I might add that each of these men is a sharpshooter."

There was a cheer from some, a raucous yell from others. He sat down.

Cris climbed into the ring, his coat over his bare shoulders.

Sam Calkins soon appeared. Cris knew when he came by the wild yells of his backers and a whispered word from Halloran, but he did not turn around or otherwise pay attention. "He'll be rough," Halloran said, "and he's great at backheeling."

"You've told me that forty times," said Cris.

The referee was a burly sergeant from the fort. He examined their fingernails and, amid loud complaints, ordered those of Calkins trimmed shorter.

Lifting his hands for silence he said, "London Prize Ring rules will hold here! A knockdown is the end of a round. Any part of the body other than the soles of the feet touching the ground is a down, and the round is ended."

He turned, glanced at the timekeeper, and at a signal from him shouted, *"Time!"*

Both men came up to the scratch and began to circle warily. Sam Calkins' body was hard with muscle, hairy, and obviously powerful. Cris Mayo's was smoother, whiter, and even more powerfully muscled in the biceps and shoulders, though Calkins was the broader.

Calkins stabbed out with a left but Mayo withdrew easily. Sam feinted, but Cris did not respond. Calkins was out to make him expend himself in the early rounds and although he had never tired during the early part of a fight, Cris was determined to make Calkins come to him. Calkins tried again with a feint, but Mayo circled away from it.

"Go get him, Sam!" somebody yelled. "He's scared."

Calkins worked in closer. He was quick. He suddenly moved forward and struck hard with a left and a right. Cris made the left miss but was slow and the right caught him a jolting blow on the chest. It hurt him none at all, but did indicate that there was no joke about Calkins' punching power.

Cris stepped back, the crowd taunting and yelling, and Calkins suddenly rushed, punching hard with both hands. Cris went into him, ducking his head to miss the blows, and catching Calkins about the waist heaved him suddenly from the ground and dropped him.

Sam was too quick. It was an attempt to end the round, but the larger man landed easily on his feet and struck hard. The blow was completely unexpected. Cris

116

had believed that the bigger man would go down into the dust and had stepped back as he let go, momentarily dropping his hands. The right Sam Calkins threw as he hit the ground flat on his feet caught Cris between the eyes and felled him in his tracks.

Wild yells came from the crowd and many cheers for Sam, who strutted back to his corner and sat down on the stool.

Cris walked back to his corner, shaking his head. The blow had dazed him, shaken him to his heels, and taught him not to take anything for granted.

A minute's rest and the bell rang, and Sam Calkins came out smiling. "This will be easy, Irish! Easy!" he said.

Cris feinted, then landed a jolting right to the ribs. It was the punch he wanted, and he ducked under a left and hooked a blow to the same spot. They closed, slugging viciously, toe to toe.

Neither gave ground and the crowd was roaring. Cris could feel his fists smashing home and suddenly his blood was up and he fell into a rhythm of punching, smashing blow after blow, he could feel himself taking punches but he did not care. He loved the fighting for the sake of it, gloried in the smash and drive of blows, the fierceness of the contest.

It was Calkins who gave ground first, and Cris drove on after him. Calkins suddenly grabbed him, backheeled him and again Cris hit the dust. He hit hard and there were taunting yells and cheers for Sam. The end of the second round.

The pace had been terrific but he felt great. The knockdown meant nothing, for this was no contest to be decided upon points. There could be only one end to this, when a man was down and unable to toe the scratch within the allotted time. And Cris felt good. He was warmed up, he was moving well, and Sam's hardest punches seemed to have only jolted him.

Sam Calkins moved in now, steadily. Cris circled to the left, away from Sam's vaunted left hand. Cris stabbed with a straight left to the mouth, but it was short. Instantly he tried the same punch, stepping in

117.

with it. The blow landed solidly, and there was a cheer from his backers as a tiny trickle of blood came from Calkins' mouth.

"First blood for Mayo!" someone shouted up on the balcony, and Calkins bulled in, landing two wicked punches to the body. He crowded Cris, landing on the body and again on the head. He smashed a right that cut Cris' ear, and Cris threw a left that all but missed, catching Sam only with the little-finger edge of his hand.

A vicious stab of pain went through him and he almost cried out. The crowd noticed and so did Sam Calkins, but neither knew what caused the pain, for Cris' maimed finger was tucked out of sight in his fist. Sam crowded in, hitting him with a right to the chin, then another right. Cris hooked a left to the ribs under the right hand, and then smashed three more to the same spot, trip-hammer style. Calkins backed off hurriedly and Cris followed him, catching him off balance with a right. It was not a hard punch but it came at the proper moment and Calkins went down in a sitting position.

Sam Calkins moved around, looking Cris over as the new round began. The idea that Cris might tire in the early rounds did not seem to be working out. Sam suddenly started in and Cris circled to the right, then stabbed a left that was short, but he kept on going in and slammed two hard rights to the ribs.

"You won't hurt me there, boy!" Sam taunted. He hit Cris with a short right that rocked him to his heels, then stabbed a left to the face and when they clinched, tried to gouge Cris' eye with a thumb. Cris smashed down with his skull on the bridge of Calkins' nose; when the bigger man drew back, he whipped over a right that staggered Calkins and sent him into the ropes.

Cris followed up and ran into a right fist that set him back on his heels and then he went on in, punching with both hands. Calkins fought back viciously; in another clinch, he backheeled Cris and as he started to fall Calkins hit hard with his right. Cris was falling away from the blow but it stunned him. He went to his knees and there was a call of "Time!"

Halloran came quickly to the center of the ring and helped Cris back to his stool.

"That's it! You got him, Sam! It's all over but the shoutin'!"

The next round came and Halloran, worried now, pushed Cris from his stool. Sam Calkins rushed in, swinging with both fists. Solid blows hit Cris, staggered him, buckled his knees, and he almost went down, then he fell into Calkins and hit him in the ribs with another punch. Hanging on, Cris fought with sheer muscular power Sam's efforts to throw him to the ground.

He hung on, struggled, then pinned Calkins' left arm under his right and spun the bigger man forward, turning him so swiftly that Calkins went up on his tiptoes, fighting for balance. Cris gave him a solid smash to the body, and a blow that glanced off Sam's head as he ducked.

Cris held his chin low and circled, his hands milling slowly before him. Sam threw his left and Cris went under it with a solid smash to the ribs that made Sam wince; rolling at the hips, Cris threw his left into the belly, and then rolling back, a right to the head. Calkins staggered and was barely able to stay up.

Suddenly and for the first time Sam Calkins seemed to realize that this was one battle he might lose. The idea was shocking, and he ripped into Cris with both hands, staggering him, smashing him with an elbow that started the blood from a cut over the right eye, then digging a wicked left into Cris' midsection.

Mayo fought back, grimly, bitterly. The bigger man rode him with his extra weight, tripped him, battered him, drove him to the edge of the ring and burned his body by twisting him against the ropes. Mayo hooked to the ear, then burying his head on Calkins' chest he backed him up with a fury of driving punches.

Calkins, butting with his head, stabbing with his thumbs, finally tripped Mayo and sent him down again.

Both men went to their corners. "How you doin'?" Pratt asked.

"All right," Cris replied, and realized suddenly that what he said was true. He had been battered, harried and driven by Calkins' punches but he was still breathing with ease, and, although bloody, was in good shape.

He walked out quickly with the call of time. Calkins feinted a left, then followed through and the punch surprised Cris and he went down again.

As the new round began, Cris Mayo deliberately threw a punch high. Calkins ducked under it, bringing his chin down for Mayo's uppercut. This had been the punch he had been warned that Sam himself would use, and as it lifted Sam from his feet and he started to fall, running in on him Cris hit him a swinging left that dropped Calkins in a heap.

As the new round began, Calkins slammed down with right fist on Mayo's wounded hand. He had finally seen the maimed finger, then. Cris ground his teeth with pain; Sam laughed, then feinted and smashed a right to the wound, then another one. They wrestled in a clinch and looking past Sam Calkins' head, Mayo saw Murray standing in Calkins' corner, grinning. His nose was bandaged, the grin showed a long gap between his teeth that hadn't been there before, and he held himself stiffly because of the broken ribs. Obviously he had told Sam about the wound.

Calkins smashed down on the hand with his elbow and Mayo cringed with the pain of it. Suddenly, a terrible rage welled up from deep inside him and burst in a sudden flame in his skull. Maddened with pain, he smashed Calkins with a right, then put both hands to the pit of the stomach. Calkins backed up, his face gray, and Cris hit him again, a hard right this time that split the skin over his left eye, then a hook to the body, another smashing right. Sam started to fall but Cris moved in, catching him around the waist with his left hand.

He hooked three short, wicked blows to the head, then pushing Calkins away he threw a high hard right to the chin. Sam Calkins' eyes glazed and he fell, and in that instant, Murray's hand came up and there was a gun in it.

There was no place to hide, nor was Cris Mayo looking for one. The impetus of his blow had swung him half around as the gun lifted and he used that impetus to throw himself straight at Murray. Murray, suddenly seeing those dreaded fists coming for him, fired much too quickly. The bullet whipped by Cris' head and Cris' right hand swung over and down.

Men, jammed in and crowded close, shoved backwards at his sudden rush. The blow descended, caught Murray on the shoulder, and he dropped to the ground, losing his hold on his gun.

Soldiers rushed in, pushing spectators aside, and the two sharpshooters sprang forward, but somehow Murray slipped through the legs of the mob and was gone.

Cris Mayo turned to the ring, but Sam Calkins was down and he was not getting up.

Chapter Thirteen

Brennan was waiting for Cris when he returned to his corner. "A fine fight, Mayo, a fine fight." From his pocket he pulled two hundred dollars. "Winner take all, and you take it fair and square."

"Thanks, Mr. Brennan."

"Are you going to fight again?"

Cris shrugged. "I may, I'd not like to say I wouldn't; but with this I can get some kind of start. You've done well for yourself, Mr. Brennan, and maybe another Irishman can do as well."

"That brings me to something else," Owen Brennan said. "I won money on you today. A good bit of it. On such occasions it's my way to do as they often do in Ireland and England. I'll share my winnings with you. I won more than five thousand dollars . . . I won't tell you how much more . . . but I am adding one thousand dollars to your two hundred."

Cris was startled. "One *thousand* dollars?" It seemed too generous to be true.

"Come to my place tomorrow, I'll have it for you. But if I were you, I'd be careful. I've seen some of the Parley outfit in town; besides, that scum Murray that tried to gun you, he won't have gone far."

Reppato Pratt dropped a hand to his gun, loosening it in the holster. "You sure 'bout that? Parley's men here?"

"Well, they used to run with that crowd, and I haven't seen some of them around Laramie until the past few days."

"I'd like a chance at Murray," growled Rep. "Cris

was right atween us an' I didn't dast shoot at the skunk. But he wants killin' real bad."

So Crispin Mayo now owned twelve hundred dollars, more money than he had seen in all the previous years of his life. To him it was a fabulous fortune, but the money brought caution. For too long he had been poor, and now this money opened doors that would otherwise be closed to him. Yet what to do, which door to choose? That needed careful thought.

Land, of course, but where? Also he must find the right horses, a good stallion and some mares. He would be wise to consult with Owen Brennan, who had come here in much the same condition as himself, and also with Colonel McClean who must know a lot about the available stock of horses in the country. If he did not know, he would be acquainted with those who would.

Cris walked back to the hotel with Reppato and Halloran. Once in their room, Pratt squatted on his heels against the wall. "Cris, you sit tight. I aim to sort of perambulate about an' see what I can uncover."

"You don't think Justin Parley has given up?" Cris asked.

"Ain't the type. He's sot in his ways, is Justin. I seen it when I was there. Silver Dick is cautious, but he's the planner too, though he don't let Parley realize it. Del Robb, well, you got to watch Del. Like Murray, he's apt to shoot most anybody for most anything."

Cris had heard this before, but he failed to see how it could matter to him now. Parley would certainly not raid the town, and when Cris left it would be to go west on the train. Barda McClean was with her father at the fort, hence safe.

He soaked his face in warm water after they had gone, holding a cloth against his swollen eye. That eye was nearly closed, and the cut above it was deep. His hands, too, were battered and swollen from the tremendous beating he had given them in pounding Calkins. The scab was knocked off the little finger, which required some rough bandaging.

Some boxing people were talking about gloves to pro-

123

tect a fighter's hands, and Cris was all for it. More often than not before a fight had gone far a fighter's hands were so swollen that he feared to hit as hard as possible. Gloves would certainly save a fighter's hands; what would happen to the opponent when a man need no longer worry about how hard he threw a punch was another thing. He had seen the kind of gloves they talked about, and some fighters were already using them in sparring sessions, and they did little if anything to save one's opponent. But they must help a fellow's hands.

It was nearly dark when he finally finished working on his battered carcass. He had found many sore places in his muscles, and more bruises than he had realized he was collecting during the fight. He had used up half a bottle of horse liniment and most of a tin of blue ointment that Rep had bought for him yesterday, and he was rather slippery and very fragrant. He lay down on the bed, hoping to catch a short nap before the others came back.

Halloran had been let off duty as one of the escort for the hunting party because of the fight, and someone was going tomorrow in his place. He could just as well have gone, Cris reflected, for the fight was over and his services were no longer required.

He was almost asleep when he thought of the bay horse. He must speak to Rep about that. He must find out whose horse it was. Anything to do with Parley was important.

He was awakened suddenly by a rapping on his door, and he opened his eyes, staring up at the ceiling for a moment, trying to recall where he was. The rapping continued and he called out, "Just a minute!" and rolled off the bed.

He was stiff and sore. Outside the light was gray, and he suddenly realized that he must have slept all night. He staggered to the door, only half awake. It was Rep, and Trooper Halloran with him.

"How're y' doin' there, boy? Still alive?" Rep asked, grinning.

"Just barely. I've got sore bones such as I never felt

124

before. That Calkins," he said, "he could really punch."

"I been gamblin' all night," said Rep, and looked abashed. "Lost both o' my horses, too, but had the sense to quit while I still had m' weepons."

Suddenly the thought came back that had bothered Cris as he was falling asleep. "Rep, while I'm thinking about it: which one of the Parley outfit owns a pretty bay horse with a black mane and tail? The brand is a straight line with another straight line above it, and three vertical lines rising from that."

"If you're going to stay out West, Cris, you better take a course in brand readin'. That's the Lazy E-Bar. Holly Barnes owns that horse, and I wish I did."

Halloran turned sharply. "Holly Barnes? That can't be. He's the guide for the generals' hunting party."

Crispin Mayo felt himself grow suddenly cold. His hands, feeling gingerly of his swollen face, stopped in their movement. The generals, all of them, going out to hunt buffalo with one of the Parley outfit for a guide. That could not be an accident.

"Hal," he asked, "how did that come about? Do you know?"

"Durrant arranged the party. You know, that railroad man who's in the dispute with Dodge over the right-of-way. Somebody told him of this Barnes who had been talking about seeing buffalo to the north near the creek, so Durrant sent a man to hire him to guide the party." Halloran stared at Rep, then Cris. "You say Barnes is one of the Parley gang? Who tried to kidnap Sherman, but got McClean?"

"That's right, Hal. Only now they have one of their men leadin' the whole outfit—Grant, Sherman, Sheridan, Haney, Dodge, everyone—taking them right where Parley wants them."

"Holly might have quit Parley," Rep said slowly. "He *might* have."

"Would you bet on it?" Cris demanded.

"No, I surely wouldn't," Rep said. "Tell you what I found out, too: a lot more of Parley's old pals are in town. His crew has growed since we tangled with it."

Cris glanced at Halloran. "We'd better be movin' fast. You get to the fort and tell 'em to roust out some of your soldier boys and go after them."

"That's just it," Halloran objected, his long face very pale. "Two patrols of twenty men each went out this morning, one east and one west along the right-of-way. There aren't more than four or five soldiers left at the fort."

Cris thought quickly. "Rep, grab your horse and head west along the track, get that patrol started to sweep north along the river or creek or whatever, to meet the generals' party. I'll go direct to them. Hal, you'd best go east and start that patrol in the right direction, or get *somebody* to go. We've got to move!"

Halloran shook his head. "Cris, you don't know what you're saying. The officers in command of those patrols have their orders. You can tell them, and they may respond and they may not. We can only tell them what we know and let them decide."

"Tell them, man! Tell them now!"

Rep was already gone. Cris Mayo belted on his six-shooter, caught up his rifle and ran down the hall. Running hurt, but he did it. At the door of the hotel he glanced swiftly left and right. Men were scattered along the streets, talking.

He lined out for Brennan's place, and seeing him, men began to straggle that way, wondering what was happening; for now Cris was a well-known figure in Laramie. Brennan had just started out the door when Cris grabbed him. "Brennan, I need a horse! The best horse you can find!" Quickly, he explained.

Brennan roared out a bull's bellow: "Hank! Joe! Hey, Swede! George! On the double!"

The men came running, others behind them. Cris heard the words, ". . . Parley. Grant and Sherman . . . ambush."

"I saw Holly on that bay horse this morning! But I never dreamed—!"

A man came around the corner of the saloon leading

126

a fine black stallion. "Cris! There you go! Ride him, and good luck!" yelled Brennan.

"I'm goin' with him!" That was Joe Hazel, one of the men Brennan had called. Other voices joined in the shout.

"Go, boy!" Brennan clapped him on the shoulder. "I'll be right behind you with thirty or forty men! Why, there's a hundred ex-Union or Confederate soldiers in town that'd fight at your hat's drop, and all law-and-order men!"

Cris sprang to the saddle and turned the black horse. He was out of town at a dead run. The river lay to the north; the hunters could be no more than an hour ahead, and their progress would be leisurely, for they were in no hurry and they had a wagon following behind.

He thought quickly. He knew only what he had seen from the railroad, but he recalled various disjointed comments from time to time about the buffalo along the river to north and south of the fort.

He came to the tracks of the hunters. Almost at once he had a shock. There were the prints of Barda's mare! He knew them well. Was she on the hunt? Or was somebody else riding the mare?

Barda . . . she must be there. And Murray was with the outlaws.

Barda. He felt a pang of fear. Barda with Murray again. . . . He looked to his rifle. It was loaded.

This was different country from that he had crossed before. It was less open, rougher, with more rock outcrops and more groves of trees. He followed the tracks of the hunting party with ease. Then suddenly he found another set that cut across them. The tracks of a fast-moving horse headed northwest.

A messenger to the outlaws?

Abruptly he decided, and leaving the trail of the hunters he turned along the route of that fast-riding horse. He rode swiftly, pausing before going over every hill to look at the country ahead of him.

127

Soon he found the trail of a number of horses, where they had met the rider Cris had been following. Now they were together and riding ahead on a course paralleling that of the hunting party. There seemed to be a great many of them.

He rode on, and he could smell dust. A mile or so away, he glimpsed a buffalo, then another. He topped out on a rise, going boldly forward. If he could do nothing else he could stampede their game, spoil the hunt, and so perhaps cause the generals to turn back.

He dropped his hand to his six-shooter. It was there, the grip on the butt a reassuring thing.

The trail dipped down into a wooded hollow and he did not like the looks of that. A man could be trapped in a place like that. He turned west, avoiding it; and as he rounded the edge, holding to the rim of the hills, he glimpsed the hunters a mile off as they, too, topped out on a rise.

He had no plan, no idea of what to do. Somewhere not far off were sixteen, eighteen, maybe twenty men or more, dedicated to the killing of all those in the hunting party, who rode unaware of the danger they faced, and in their midst, Barda McClean. The thought sickened him.

Crispin Mayo sat the black horse and looked carefully around, his eyes searching every bit of cover. His tongue touched his dry lips and he tapped the horse with his heels, moving forward at a slow walk.

He had the feeling that he was watched, that he was not alone. The hair prickled on the back of his neck. There were Indians in this land, but these men were worse than Indians, they were savages of another, more evil kind. Renegades. Butchers. . . .

Before him the hill sloped down and there was a narrow path, a game trail, that led through trees and up the farther side. He hesitated, but saw no way around without riding too far from the people he was trying to warn.

Three buffalo appeared from nowhere before him, crossing his trail at a trot, then another. There were trees along the slope of the hill below him and on an impulse he swung the black horse down into those trees. There he pulled up and lifted the rifle.

Four men rode up the trail following the buffalo, and one of them was Murray.

Chapter Fourteen

The position that Cris Mayo had taken offered but little cover, and any glance in his direction might reveal him. He sat very still, whispering just a little to the stallion, praying that it would make no sound.

The four riders went on past, followed by their dust cloud, yet still he waited, his heart pounding. He needed no one to tell him how desperate his situation was. The men who were seeking to ambush the generals had equally as much reason to kill him; Murray had an even greater reason.

To the southwest were the Medicine Bow Mountains; nearer was Laramie Creek, and the hunting party of generals had ridden up toward its waters.

Cris knew nothing about the creek, or this land in which he found himself. Evidently Murray and the three other outlaws had been a scouting party, with the main group lying somewhere near the creek and the buffalo. No doubt Holly Barnes was even now guiding the generals closer to the river, and Cris could do nothing. They would be closely watched and if he attempted to join them and warn them he would be cut down at once by the outlaws.

He walked his horse cautiously up the slope and into the open. From the crest of the ridge, without skylining himself, he could see for miles. Not far off he saw a good-sized bunch of buffalo. Suddenly the idea came to him . . . suppose he could stampede them across the path of the hunting party? Or even drive them close enough to be seen, and therefore to be a potential target? Might that help? Well, it just might.

Dropping down off the ridge he rode fast, keeping to low ground between two lines of hills. When he came up, a few minutes later, he saw the buffalo not two hundred yards away. He started toward them, walking his horse.

One big old bull lifted a ponderous head and stared at him. The beast took two hesitant steps toward him, then wheeled and started back in the other direction. Cris walked the black horse toward them, and uneasily they began to move away. The Parley outfit were nowhere in sight, no doubt concentrating all their attention on the hunting generals.

He circled warily, for he knew nothing of buffalo except from the casual talk on the train, not all of which he remembered; and some comments made by Reppato Pratt; and the raging tide of them that had come at the red shack in the night, the night when he'd turned them. Cris Mayo wanted no stampede, only an alternative target that might lead the generals away from the ambush, which he felt sure would be baited with buffalo.

If he could manage it, he might defeat Parley's crowd without a fight. He had no urge for a shooting match. Actual combat was a last resort. There were men out there whose lives were precious to their country, and there was Barda.

Cris pulled up and waited, watching the buffalo moving away. When they ran it was with a queer, loping gait, their heads bobbing, their long beards often touching the grass. Slowly, then, he walked his horse along a wide front, his appearance enough to keep the animals moving on.

The air was very clear, with almost no wind. Cris stood in his stirrups and tried to see beyond the low hills to where the hunting party might be.

There was nothing . . . only the shimmer of the clear, sunlit air, only the stillness. Somewhere a meadowlark called, and far overhead a buzzard swung in lazy loops, watching for what might develop.

He dismounted and walked on, leading the black horse. The buffalo he had started were moving across the line of march on which he had glimpsed the hunt-

131

ing party, and if they continued to move would offer an open target, away from the creek bottom where Parley's men must be waiting.

The wind was from him toward the buffalo and they drifted away as he approached, but because he was moving slowly, they did likewise. Where were Parley's men? He studied each fold in the hills, knowing that they were within half a mile of him, probably less, and that any one of them would be willing to kill him on sight . . . only now they would be apt to hold their fire for fear of warning the generals.

Somewhere behind were Owen Brennan and his followers, whoever he had found in Laramie where there were many veterans of the war from both sides. Brennan would be riding by now.

Cris mounted again and began moving his horse forward, pushing the buffalo a little. Suddenly, some distance off, he saw the generals' party ride out of a draw and pull up. He could see the sun glisten on the flanks of their horses, but was too far off to make out details or numbers.

He cantered forward toward the buffalo, and after a look at him, they swung their big heads and moved off. Cris had been visible long enough for them to feel no great alarm at his presence, but they moved now at a more rapid pace, as he did.

A dozen were trotting . . . twenty or more, with others starting. They had been scattered upon the grass, now they bunched a little. He stared at the generals' party, shielding his eyes against the sun. They appeared to be hesitating, debating whether to follow the guide or try for this new lot who were coming at them.

The buffalo before him veered sharply to the north, shying from a crease in the hills that must be a coulee or draw. He took his rifle in his hands. His lips felt dry . . . well, he knew where some of the devils were, anyway. He started to swing wide of the spot, and three men appeared, as if from the ground.

They were on foot and not thirty yards away. What impelled him to do so he never could guess, but suddenly he kicked the black horse in the ribs and drove at them.

His action was totally unexpected, and the horse was in a dead run before they realized he was coming at them, not running away. He leaned out, taking aim at the farthest one, and firing on the jump. He missed . . . but he worked the lever, fired again, and then swung the rifle butt. And that time he did not miss.

He felt the shock of the blow clear to his spine, and at the same moment a gun went off almost in his ear and the ravine opened before him. He cut the black sharply away along the rim, glancing back. Two men were down but one of them was getting up, having either been upset by the horse or tripped in his haste to get out of its way. One of them was lifting a rifle, but at that instant the land dipped and Cris went into a low place and swung in and out among scattered juniper.

He heard whining bullets . . . or thought he did. At least he heard the reports, and then he was down even lower and making time away from them. When he finally topped out on the far side of the shallow place he was a quarter of a mile away and the men had disappeared. All but the one he had hit with the gun butt, who still lay, a dark spot on the brown-gray grass.

Turning his horse, he saw that the creek was before him. Somewhere among those trees were the rest of Parley's men. He pulled up among some rocks and deadfalls and tying his horse in a sheltered place, walked quickly forward.

He did not know what to do, but they were somewhere in the brush down there and he wanted to smoke them out. He checked his ammunition . . . plenty. He looked down into the trees below and could see nothing, and much as it went against the grain to waste ammunition by throwing lead at an invisible target, he knew he must do something more to warn the generals, at least to move them away from the ambush.

He heard a voice raised down there in some kind of command. He knelt behind a fallen tree and resting his rifle barrel across it he began a searching fire into the

133

woods. He had no target, only the necessity of stirring them up and creating a warning racket, so he fired, elevated the muzzle an inch or so, fired again. With deliberation he put ten shots into the area, searching along the patch of trees, hoping to get some action.

At the sound of the firing he saw from the tail of his eye the hunting party. They seemed to stop . . . he could imagine them swearing at the "damned fool" who was frightening the game, though as a matter of fact it only moved the buffalo toward them.

Justin Parley had held his file of men ready for a charge. Talk about Stuart, would they? Or Forrest? Or this upstart Yankee Custer? He would show them what a cavalry charge was like, and wipe them out in the process.

The frustration of his original plans had been gnawing at him. It had seemed a simple, dramatic gesture to grab Sherman, torture and kill him, and notify the world that he had avenged Atlanta. Then the added chance to kill all three, Grant, Sherman and Sheridan, had come. He would be a hero . . . a *hero!*

"Major," it was Watkins, a tough Arkansas rebel, "that damn Irishman is movin' the buffalo!"

"What?" Parley's daydreams of heroism, of the day when he would be the toast of all unreconstructed Southerners, were interrupted. "What was that?"

"The Irishman . . . the fighter. He's movin' the buffalo."

"Kill him!" Parley snapped. "You, Watkins, and Murray and Hardt. Get out there and stop him. Kill him!"

They had gone on foot for better shooting, but in the meantime Cris Mayo had ridden nearer, and their sudden emergence had put him right on top of them; and then, instead of running, the idiot had charged them.

Hardt was down out there, probably dead. Watkins and Murray, bitter with anger at themselves, their luck and Cris Mayo, dropped into the ravine. Watkins had been knocked down by a glancing blow from the horse's

134

shoulder. Shaken, he had stumbled into the brush, following Murray.

Murray had scrambled back for the rifle he had dropped, then run to the sheltering brush. "Where'd he go?" he demanded of Watkins.

"Disappeared," Watkins growled irritably. "He was there, then he was gone. What's the matter with him, anyway? Is he crazy?"

"He ain't crazy," Murray replied shortly. "He's just got more nerve than any one man should have. That damn mick would charge Hell with a bucket o' water!"

Parley was ready. The hunting party would come no closer with the buffalo moving as they were, but they were less than half a mile off and partially screened by scattered juniper and brush. He would walk his horses the first couple of hundred yards, trot for a hundred, then charge.

"Ready!" His voice rang out. He lifted a sword. "Ready," he repeated, wishing he could remember the proper commands. In the irregular outfit he had served with, such commands were rarely used, but he would have liked to know them now. *"Rea—!"*

A bullet kicked dust thirty yards off and the hard crack of the rifle sounded close. A second bullet struck a tree and spat bark, another thunked into the dirt almost at his horse's feet.

"Charge!" Parley shouted. It was the first word that came to him, and not at all the one he wanted. The whole line of horsemen surged forward, up the bank of the coulee and into the scattered juniper and sagebrush beyond.

Mayo heard the wild shout, and the next instant the riders came boiling out of the coulee, faced in the opposite direction. There must have been twenty-five of them. Whirling around, Mayo got off one quick shot, saw a rider fall, and then his gun clicked on an empty chamber.

Desperately, he began to reload. They were pulling away! He whipped up the rifle and pumped five shots after them, five that had no effect, and his gun was

135

empty again. With quick fingers he again slid in cartridges, kneeling, determined this time to load the gun completely.

It was reloaded and he started to stand when he heard a footfall. He sprang up, turned, heard the bellow of a gun and a wild, angry, triumphant yell. "Got him!" And then the gun roared again.

He felt himself falling, threw out a hand to stay his fall but it caught nothing; tripped by the log, he fell over it and struck the side of his head hard on the ground beyond. He heard running feet and yelling, and he threw himself over into the ravine.

He was hurt, how badly he did not know, but his mind was confused and filled with panic. He had to get away, *get away!*

He hit some brush, pitched through it, struck heavily on something hard and then fell clear. He brought up with a jolt in the soft mud near a stream. He tried to get up, fell, and crawled. Half blind with dirt and mud, he saw a dark hole before him and scrambled toward it.

It was no hole . . . no safe place, only a dark hollow in the brush where some animal had crawled. He scrambled along it, his breath coming in great gasps. Above him on the bank over which he had fallen he heard shouting and swearing. *"Get him,* damn it! *Kill him!"*

He heard running feet. He suddenly emerged from the animal crawlway, staggered to his feet and lunged through the trees, bumping first one and then another. He felt a stabbing pain in his side, but whether from a bullet or simply exhaustion he could not say. His head was opening and shutting with fierce spasms of torment.

He fell down, got up. He had lost his rifle back there when he fell over the log. His horse was there, too. In the hands of the renegades by now, surely.

He ran a few steps, butted into a tree and grabbed wildly at the trunk to keep himself from falling. He turned, looking back. He could see nothing but leaves and brush. He ran on, desperately wanting a hole. Somewhere he heard a yell, then a volley of shots, but none of them came close to him.

136

Suddenly, running at full tilt, he saw the ravine narrow before him, a rocky place, solid rock underneath. He ran at the opening, saw the rock vanish almost before his eyes and he was on the lip of a cliff, a dry waterfall!

He tried to slow down, to stop himself, but his impetus was too great. He felt himself go over, his fingers clawing for the rocks. He caught a corner of stone and for a moment thought he had saved himself, but the rock pulled loose and he fell, struck some brush, crashed through, and the last thing he knew was a faint circle of light above and then darkness closing in.

A half mile away, Brennan with thirty riders pulled up on the brow of a low hill. They could see nothing. Off toward the mountains he heard the bark of a gun from the hunters.

"Well," he said, "they're still—" At that moment Parley's men came up the bank in their wild charge, which had started too soon and too far from their objective.

"Take 'em, men!" Brennan slapped spurs to his horse and started forward. And they opened fire.

The shock of the unexpected flank attack was too much. Parley's men, poorly disciplined at least, broke before it. Brennan's hard riders, most of them cavalry veterans of the Civil and Indian Wars, relishing this sudden call to action, charged into the fleeing renegades with flaming guns.

In a moment, it was over. Half a dozen men were on the ground. Several fled, barely clinging to their saddles, and Silver Dick, one of the last ones up the bank in the ill-considered charge, had turned sharply at the first shot and gone back into the river bottom, Del Robb beside him.

There was a crashing in the brush, and Murray ran out on foot, eyes bulging with anger. "Where'd he go?" he yelled. "Did you see that mick?"

"Forget it, Murray! Get your horse and come on! We've been hit . . . hard!"

Turning sharply, within fifty yards of the dry waterfall over which Mayo had fallen, they rode back up the ravine under the cover of the trees. On the way they picked up Watkins and two more. Gradually others joined them until there were a dozen or so.

There was no sign of Justin Parley.

Chapter Fifteen

Holly Barnes looked nervously toward the sound of the shooting. What had happened to Parley? He had kept the hunting group as close to the river as he dared insist, and then that other bunch of buffalo had drifted nearer, diverting them from the route he planned. And now the shooting . . . what had gone wrong?

Suddenly he wanted to be away from here. He wanted to be riding, and riding fast, yet there was no excuse he could give for leaving. He had contracted as a guide, and if there was still an attack, and he had tried to leave—

It could be a hanging matter. Grant seemed pleasant enough, and Sheridan also, but Sherman was a hard man and one given to asking questions.

Colonel Seymour rode up, accompanied by McClean. "Barnes, what's all that shooting about?"

"I don't know, Colonel. Maybe some cowboys play-actin', tryin' to scare you, more'n likely. You know how it is, that would make a great story after you boys left the country, how they scared you-all."

Seymour was irritated, "We are not scared, as you put it, Barnes. We are not at all scared. Ride on!"

Barnes wet his lips. "Colonel, I think—"

"Barnes, we came to hunt. So let us hunt."

Barnes glanced again over the bland, unassuming prairie, broken with occasional rocks and patches of timber in the lowlands. It told him nothing. Once he thought he glimpsed a dust cloud.

What was going on over there? What had happened to Parley?

He led the group on toward the buffalo, then hung

back as they moved out to the hunt. He wanted to get away, but for some reason McClean seemed more interested in him than in the hunt. Did McClean know him? How could he? When McClean had been a prisoner, Holly had been in Laramie scouting for information.

He was nervous, and he was afraid it showed. McClean was no fool, and the colonel was watching him. Somehow, too, McClean always seemed to have that rifle in his hands pointed in Holly's direction.

Suddenly Barda McClean came riding up. "Father! Look!"

McClean turned. A party of horsemen were approaching. Colonel McClean, who had the memory of a cowboy when it came to horses, recognized several that he had seen at the fort or in town. He took up his glass and leveled it. Brennan, that saloonkeeper from town, what was he doing out here? Singleton, Cooney, storekeeper Clyde Dixon . . . what was this?

"Let's ride over, Seymour. There's something wrong about this."

Swinging their mounts, Barda beside them, they rode swiftly toward the approaching band.

Behind them Holly Barnes took one look. That was none of his outfit. About a hundred yards away there was a shallow draw; he rode at an angle, then suddenly did a vanishing act into the draw.

It had been a crazy idea anyway, trying to kill all those generals. Why had he ever let himself get into a stupid thing like that?

Holly Barnes was not an enlightened man, but he had a good bit of practical sense when he settled down to use it, and at this moment it told him that Nevada was a beautiful, extraordinary land uniquely situated to benefit by his talents, a land that was waiting, gasping for his arrival . . . an arrival too long delayed.

"If you keep ridin', Holly," he told himself, "you can camp thirty miles from here, and the sooner you get to that there camp, the better!"

Crispin Mayo of County Cork, of Skibbereen, Clonakilty and Rosscarbery, opened his eyes upon a star. It was a single star, straight above him, and there was no other he could see. For several minutes he lay perfectly still, hoping the star would not go away; and when it did not, he moved his head.

His neck was stiff, and his head felt thick and heavy. He rolled over onto his face and pushed himself up to hands and knees. He was one great lump of pain. Memory came back slowly. He had been shot at from close up, he had been running in blind panic for the first time in his life, and he had taken a bad fall. That must have been hours ago.

His fingers closed on sand . . . a creek bed, no doubt. He remembered of a sudden that he had fallen off a dry waterfall, and he thought he'd landed in some brush. He must have crashed through the brush to this sand.

It was night, and whatever had been about to happen when he'd blacked out had happened long since. That had been around noon. And now it was dark, or all but dark—the sky was a cobalt blue just shading into sapphire.

He had lost his horse and rifle.

His side felt stiff; he touched it and found dried blood caked with sand. His shirt was stuck to his side. When he got up, he stood uncertainly, testing himself for what else might be wrong.

He *had* been shot before he fell, then. The wound in the side could have come only from a bullet. It didn't feel too serious, just stiff and aching. He was bruised and sore all over from his fall, and he felt shaky as a leaf in high wind. But his head was the worst.

He stumbled over to a polished boulder and sat down, touching his skull gently here and there. It hurt badly, but he could not find a wound. Not a gunshot, then. The fall . . . no, the two falls! He'd gone over that log when he'd been shot, and hit the side of his head hard on ground or rock. Then he'd panicked, a thing so foreign to his nature that he could not understand it.

He had run like a hare; he, Cris Mayo, who'd have died before he disgraced himself so. He felt his natural pride drain way to leave him hollow, a husk, a coward.

141

He'd run till the dry waterfall dropped him into blackness. Maybe he'd hit his head again that time, to sleep so long?

They did say that a good knock on the skull could send a man crazy for a time, so that he'd do daft things. Cris took a long breath. That must have been it. He surely wasn't the bravest of men, but by the powers he wasn't a man who ran from danger, either! It had been the terrible blow. It had addled his wits.

They seemed to be returning to him now. He got to his feet. His hand went to his holster: his six-gun was there, miraculously. The cool butt in his palm was reassuring.

His eyes were growing accustomed to the darkness and he saw an opening in the canopy of brush that showed light. Bent over, he went through and stood in the open, under a low-riding moon. He was on the bottom of a dry creek bed with high rock walls. The waterfall over which he had dropped was behind him and no more than fifteen feet in height. Still, if he'd gone down that drop and smacked his thick Irish skull a second time, it was sure little wonder that he'd slept for hours!

He heard no sound. He sat again, studying the walls. He must get out of here, but he had no desire to pitch over another cliff in the process. There was a lot of broken brush and branches littering the place, and one of the latter he chose for a staff. Limping, he started down the creek.

It was Murray who had shot him, he was certain of that from his remembrance of the roaring voice he'd heard; and Murray was a vengeful man who might still be prowling this neighborhood looking for him.

Cris had walked only a few yards when he found the walls of the ravine no longer sheer. Yet he was also finding new pains in his battered carcass. He stopped and rested again.

His eyes were used to the early night now and he could see the dark shapes of rocks, clumps of brush, and along the side of one wall a narrow trail going up . . . probably made by deer, buffalo or wild horses.

He started hobbling along. His right leg hurt abominably, not broken, he was sure, but no doubt badly bruised. His maimed left hand throbbed, so did his head. He looked up the narrow, angling path. There was no danger in it, but he dreaded the effort needed. Yet he started on, and after a while came out on top.

There were many stars. The sky was clear, the lifting moon just past the full. His eyes sought out and recognized the shapes around him. How far was he from Laramie or Fort Sanders? The fort was closer, he believed, but his sense of direction was twisted. He found the North Star easily enough. It seemed to be in the wrong place, yet he knew it must be he himself who was turned around.

He waited a minute, leaning on his staff and trying to place himself. Was his rifle still on the ground back there? And the black horse? If they had not found that fine stallion he might still be tied there, in that hidden place!

He hobbled along, swearing a little at his own near-helplessness, but the movements gradually came easier as his stiffened muscles loosened up. How long had he been lying back there? He looked at the stars, trying to estimate time by the Big Dipper.

If he was judging correctly it was about nine. That meant nine hours lost in unconsciousness, indeed, as he'd guessed by the moon's height. He found his way to the place he had hidden in to send his searching bullets down the ravine. He could see little there, but he felt around in the darkness with his toe.

Nothing. He moved to the log over which he had fallen. They must have been right on top of him, and then there had been the attack, he thought, recollecting the spate of firing. Had they followed Parley? And what had happened out there on the buffalo range? Were the generals dead? Or Barda McClean?

Suddenly his eye caught a gleam of starlight on metal. He dropped his staff and reached down and picked up his rifle. Next to it lay his hat. He put it on his sore head gingerly.

Luck . . . pure luck. Now, if only his horse was still there!

Why not? He had tied the knot pretty tight, and the hiding place had been good. Moreover, they had been in a hurry, thinking only of killing him and getting on with their dirty plot.

Everything was different in the dark. He listened. Far off, in a tree near the stream, he could hear a mockingbird, awake for some reason at this hour. Had it been disturbed by someone besides himself?

He crouched near a boulder, wiping the dirt from his rifle with his hands. If the muzzle were stopped up, the gun might explode in his hands. He wanted to tap it against a boulder but worried about the sound it would make, an unnatural sound in the night, if anybody was listening.

He felt on the ground for a small twig, found one, tested the gun muzzle. It seemed to be clear of obstruction.

He knew about where his horse had been. By now of course it might have broken free and gone back to Laramie. Then Brennan would probably be hunting him by daylight or soon after. But would he? How well did he know Brennan, after all, and had not Brennan one thousand dollars he had promised to Cris Mayo?

He shrugged. He had a feeling that Brennan would be looking, when he knew that his prizefighter had vanished.

Cris was wary of the night. How many times had he crouched so, and listened? Not only for the gamekeeper, either, for there had been other enemies. He listened, straining his ears for the slightest sound.

Nothing. . . .

He straightened to his feet and carrying the rifle under his arm he limped toward where he believed his horse to be. Yet all was different. Landmarks seen by day are too often invisible by night, and the trees he had selected yesterday had merged with each other in the blackness. He went a short way, moving as quietly as he could, then sat down again, partly to rest and partly to get the outline of trees and hills against the sky.

Suddenly, he heard the faintest of sounds . . . some-

144

thing was out there. His horse? Murray? Brennan? Rep, maybe?

He waited, listening for a repetition of the sound. There was none. He tried to place it in his mind . . . a click of hoof on stone? The bump of a rifle against a branch? After a moment he moved on, trying desperately to make no sound.

He stopped again. He had heard nothing, yet he was sure something was out there, and not just his horse. Irish nerves are sensitive to unheard things in the night.

Something was out there, waiting.

He moved into the shadow of a juniper and dropped his right hand to his six-gun and slid the thong from the hammer. Could he get it out fast enough? Rep had said that the secret was not speed, but just to be sure that you got it out, levelled it steadily, and fired. To take that extra whisper of time . . . his uncle had said the same thing about a rifle. Had he loaded his rifle, after emptying it that day? He couldn't remember. If only his blasted head didn't throb so!

He stood thinking. He had been able to see into the ravine from the place where he'd left his horse. Or he had before he dismounted, which was different. Yet he was sure that right at this moment his horse should be within sixty yards or so of where he stood. *If* the horse was still there.

Suppose Murray was stalking him? Suppose Murray had found the stallion, left it where it was, and just pulled back to wait for him?

Then the instant he untied the horse, Cris would take a slug through the spine.

The thought had no appeal.

He touched his six-shooter again. Murray and two others had been hunting him. He had nailed down one of them, certainly; if that man was alive he was in no condition to be poking around in the dark. But what of Murray and the other one? Had they ridden on with Parley?

The night was still. Scarcely a leaf moved as Cris Mayo stood by the juniper and listened. Then finally he heard a faint stirring, not far off, a small rattle—the sound of a horse mouthing his bit. He was closer than he'd believed.

Lifting a foot, he placed it gently down, making no noise. He moved forward a step, and then another.

Something stirred faintly on the left; and the rattle of the bit had come from his *right* front. He listened, straining for the slightest sound. He took a sudden step to his right, tested the ground and put his foot down gently, then shifted his weight.

Above him a nighthawk dipped and circled, then whisked away through the trees. All was white and still in the moonlight, every object standing out in bold relief, yet the shapes were strange to him. The boulders cast shadows, as did the trees, shadows as dark as themselves, giving them weird, malformed aspects never seen by day.

Somewhere down the slope a pebble rattled. Natural? Or disturbed by something . . . somebody?

He could feel the trickles of perspiration despite the coolness of the night. Who was it who lurked nearby? He dared not simply shoot, for it might be Rep or Brennan, somebody searching for him but wary of Parley's men.

Cris Mayo took another careful step to his right. He was still shadowed by junipers, but this would be his last such move. He squatted down, peering ahead.

The black horse should be less than sixty feet downslope and to the right. He was closer than he had at first believed . . . or had the rattle of the bit come from another horse?

He eased the rifle into his two hands after checking his revolver again. He was growing irritated by the suspense, the waiting. He knew it was a dangerous feeling, for it might betray him into a move that would be the death of him; yet he had no idea whether there really *was* somebody out there. The imagination can play tricks, aided by natural movements of the earth and of animals. Sounds that occur all day long may be noticed only in the stillness of night. But pains and aches that wrench at a man from toes to crown, they make him impatient.

He took up a small stone from near his foot and tossed it thirty feet back up the slope. He heard it hit, then rattle as it rolled down among rocks. Silence.

There was a gap of a dozen feet between himself and the next juniper downslope and to the right. He moved, lunging suddenly from the ground and throwing himself toward the tree.

He was seeking only another protective shadow, but what he smashed into was something quite different. He had started down in his crouching position and moved low and fast. His brogans grated on pebbles and then his shoulder hit hard against an obstacle that gave way before him. A hand clawed at his face, and a man rolled onto his back, into the open moonlight.

The man he had seen with Murray!

Knocked sprawling, Watkins lost his grip on his gun and it fell. He scrambled for it and Cris Mayo shot from where he crouched. No more than eight feet away and the rifle in his hands, he simply fired. And the rifle *had* been loaded, despite his worries. Watkins grunted, started to rise up. "Damn you!" he said clearly, and then he fell.

Instantly a bullet struck within inches of Cris Mayo. He ran, crouched, fired, levered his rifle, fired again. Then he charged directly at the hidden marksman, working the lever as he moved. A gun blasted almost in his face and the stab of flame half-blinded him, but gripping the rifle in his two hands he took a wicked jab with the muzzle into the darkness where the flame had shown.

The gun struck, a heavy rocking blow to a man's upper body. Mayo heard the man grunt, fall, then scramble up and run. He shot, blindly, for the figure was indistinct and moving. He was sure it was Murray . . . and sure he had missed him.

Turning, he ran back along the slope toward his horse. If it was there. Watkins still lay sprawled motionless, ungainly in the moonlight.

Ducking into the small hollow where the black indeed stood, Cris tugged at the knot of the reins. It failed to give, evidently pulled tighter by the stallion's movements. Slipping the rifle under an arm, he started to struggle with the knot.

"There now!" The tone was quiet, amused. "Just stay right there, young man. I am really a very fine shot, and I have you silhouetted against the sky. If I missed you, I might shoot the horse, and neither of us want that, do we?"

Cris held very still. "Why shoot me? I don't even know you, mister. A couple of men just tried to steal my horse, and—"

"It won't do, Mr. Mayo. It just won't do at all. You see, I know you. I know who you are and all about you. Most important, I have someone you are interested in."

"You have someone? I don't know what you mean."

The laugh was almost pleasant. "Of course, you do not, Mr. Mayo. Of course not. You see, I have Barda McClean."

"*You* have her? Who are you?"

Again the laugh. "I am Major Justin Parley, Mr. Mayo. I believe you know the name?"

Chapter Sixteen

Crispin Mayo stood very still. He knew little of the man he faced other than that he had commanded the renegades, and that now he said he had Barda McClean. Cris spoke carelessly. "I have heard of you, Major Parley. That you have Barda McClean, I do not believe."

"You should believe it. It is because of you that I have her. When you did not return to Laramie, she assumed that you were lying injured out here, and she came looking for you."

That would be like her, of course. A brave, fearless, reckless girl, that one. Cris felt his stomach muscles tighten. Parley was here, and he would scarcely be alone . . . how many were with him? And if he had Barda, where was she?

"You do not believe she would come for you? Oh, Mr. Mayo! You are mistaken. You misjudge the lady. She would come, she did come, in fact. I envy you, Mr. Mayo. It is not often one incurs the regard of such a lovely lady to that extent."

"If you have harmed her—!"

"Come, come, Mr. Mayo! I am not a savage. Miss McClean is a lady, and I am a Southern gentleman."

"In Ireland we have heard of Southern gentlemen," Cris spoke carefully, "and it is a fine thing to be one, sir. I envy you."

Parley was pleased, and it sounded in his voice. "I regret that we are enemies, Mr. Mayo. The Irish nobility is very ancient."

"It is that, sir. But I was never your enemy. I was attacked, and I defended myself. And then Miss McClean

149

asked me to help rescue her father. What else could I have done?"

Justin Parley, renegade or not, fancied himself a gentleman. He considered himself a model of chivalry, so the right way to handle this would be to accept him at his own measure and see that he lived up to it. Cris went on. "I would not have worried had I known you were a gentleman, sir. All them that travel these Western plains are not your sort."

"Put down your weapon," Parley said. "I think we understand each other."

"We do, I am sure, but you'll not be mindin' if I keep the gun? It reassures me, sort of."

There was a moment of silence and then a faint footfall behind him, and holding the rifle elbow-high he turned sharply and struck viciously sidelong with the butt.

A man had come in behind him and lifted a rifle with both hands to club him. The sudden turn and the smashing blow in the ribs brought the man down.

There was a thud, a moaning grunt, and silence.

"What was that?" Parley demanded.

"I think somebody fell," Cris said innocently, and eased a step forward. "Sounded like it was behind me."

Parley stood somewhere in shadow, as did Cris himself. "Get your horse," Parley said. "Miss McClean is at my camp. I am sure she will be pleased to see you."

"I don't believe, savin' your presence, sir, that you have a camp," Cris replied, "and I'm not much in the mood for travel."

How many were out there? Or was there anyone now but Justin Parley and himself? There had been the man behind him, of course, but—

"It was my thought you'd be far from here," Cris said, "for the vigilantes will be out again by daylight, and the Army, too. There's two patrols out, you know . . . the two that guard the railroad, they've both turned this way and before mornin' they'll be closing in on you likewise." He had no idea whether this was true, but it seemed logical.

"Yes?" Parley's tone was higher. Cris was sure that

Parley was suddenly worried. "And why should you warn me of this?"

"Look, Major, I don't want to get myself caught in a shootin' among the lot of you. I have no part in this fight. I've been in your country no more than two months and I know nothing of your fights or frolics. You say you have Barda McClean. What you hope to gain by capturing a girl who is just out of school I don't know, but my feeling is that you'd better leave her with me and scatter out. Just scatter out and run. The odds are too high against you."

"You make it sound very simple." There was irritation and impatience in the voice. Cris had an idea that Parley was waiting for that man to come up behind him. "We will keep Miss McClean, and you."

Cris took a step backward, very gently. The man he had hit was stirring. Evidently the blow with the butt of the rifle over the heart had hurt him, but not enough. Stooping, Cris stripped him of his pistol and knife, and picked up the fallen rifle. He took off the man's cartridge belt and as the fellow began to rise, hit him a smashing blow on the head with the pistol barrel.

"What was that?" Parley demanded.

"A skull gettin' cracked," Cris replied mildly. "Somebody tried comin' up behind me. I didn't much care for it."

"Drop your gun," Parley said harshly, "and come out with your hands up!"

Cris shifted his weight, then crouched, holding the fallen man's pistol. "Like the divil I will," he said. "You start shootin' when you're ready, Major." The time for all that gentlemen stuff was past.

There was silence, absolute silence. Uneasily, he waited, then lowered one knee to the ground and very gently worked his way back. He was well in the shadow, and there was another tree close behind him. His toe found a sort of gully a few inches deep, a place where water had run off the top of the hill. That would deepen as it went down, he decided.

The black horse stomped a foot, restless and wanting to be moving.

Cris took a chance and rose suddenly, stepped to the horse and felt for the knot. He had started untying it before, and now it took but a couple of seconds. He heard no sound. Parley might have slipped away when his trap failed, but there wasn't a guarantee of that.

Thrusting the spare pistol behind his belt and holding both rifles, he stepped into the saddle and turned the black horse quickly down the gully he had found.

Behind him there was a shot. It must have missed by several feet, and then he was riding swiftly away, leaning forward the better to see the trail. Soon he was in the bottom of a sandy wash and his horse made almost no sound.

He was away, and Parley must have had only the one man with him, or else for some reason they were afraid to shoot. The one shot had been fired by Parley himself, Cris was sure, and probably in a fit of anger. But he was assuming things that he did not know.

The wash led south and widened rapidly, spilling out on a plain of sagebrush with occasional juniper.

Parley had obviously attempted to bluff him into surrender, and when that failed, withdrew . . . but for what purpose? Cris could not see how he would be of any value to the renegades. He was of no importance to anyone but himself. Yet the thought that they might have Barda rankled. He did not believe it, but it was possible.

He followed the wash to the plain and rode across the open toward a clump of trees on a slope. Warily, he scouted the area, but his horse showed no interest so he rode into the trees. Picketing the black on a patch of grass, he leaned back against a cottonwood to rest, watching the way he had come.

He was well armed. He now had two rifles, two pistols, and a knife, as well as the extra ammunition he had taken from the man he'd knocked out. If they came at him, he was ready.

He rested his much-abused body for half an hour, then got up, put on his hat and went to his horse. He saddled up, fussing over the horse a little as the black seemed to like attention, and then, aware now of

152

hunger, checked the saddlebag. Unexpectedly he found that Brennan had had two sandwiches, thick with bread and beef, put into the saddlebag along with an apple. Seated where he could watch the moonlit country around, he ate one of the sandwiches and the apple. He was hungry enough to eat the other sandwich, but he had no idea how long he would be without food, so decided to keep it a bit longer.

He rode south into rougher country. Topping out on a rise, he studied the land about him. In all that vast expanse he could see nothing.

The logical thing was to return to Fort Sanders or Laramie and get the latest news, find out what had happened.

Off to the west the country was rougher still, and rising into higher mountains. He circled around, hoping to pick up the trail of Barda McClean, but there was a confusion of tracks, some of them yesterday's, some old. There was nothing to do but head for Fort Sanders.

Reluctantly, he took his bearings by the stars and turned the black, which was in good shape and seemed to thrive on Wyoming grass. Parley's comments rankled. Did he really have Barda McClean? Or had he invented that? And why, of all people, would they care about *him?* He was nobody, save to himself.

He buttoned his coat. There was a chill in the air that let him know he had best be planning for cold weather, and him with no place to stay. Riding around on fine horses playing at soldier or scout was well enough if it helped honest people, but it brought him no money.

Of course, he had twelve hundred dollars. A goodly sum, well worth the pounding he'd taken, and sufficient to start in business if he was so minded. He might buy a few horses and—

Something tugged at his hat and then he heard the bark of a rifle, and he wheeled his horse over and charged into the nearest gully. He had no idea where the shot had come from, only that somebody had fired, and he headed for the lowest ground he could find.

He raced his horse into the gully, galloped a fast

hundred yards, saw a canyon branching off and turned sharply into it, going back toward where he'd just come from. The floor of the ravine was sandy; he slowed his horse to a walk, holding one of the rifles, the newly captured one, in his hands. The other was in the saddle scabbard.

He was wary, but if they pursued him they would likely head on down the gully, and not double back as he had done. He was rounding the corner of the rocks when he heard a hoof strike stone. There was no chance to turn, to swerve, to do anything, for the black was moving forward quicker than he could check it.

The sound had given him an instant of warning and his rifle was up when he turned the corner.

There were three riders before him, and one of them was just shouting, "I had him dead to rights! I had him spang in my sights, and I tell you he's got to be dead!"

Crispin Mayo knew only one way to fight: to win. He took his one instant of advantage and opened fire.

The riders were practically at arm's length and he shot the speaker out of his saddle, and then went on firing as rapidly as he could work the lever, too fast for accuracy but good for spooking the enemy. One of the riders slapped spurs to his horse and jumped it past Mayo, firing wildly as he dashed by. The heat of the bullet flicked his cheek ... or he thought it did ... and Cris shot at the third man, who had turned his horse in its tracks and was going up the canyon at a dead run.

Twice he fired at that man, more carefully, and saw him jerk and throw up his hands, but somehow with a rider's instinct he stayed in the saddle.

Wheeling the black, Cris tore back to see what had become of the rider who had raced by him down the canyon; and the man and horse were out of sight, only dust lingering in the air.

The moon was an hour higher now, flooding the land with light. Turning back, he looked at the riderless horse. A chestnut with a somewhat lighter mane and tail, a handsome horse. The rider lay on the rocks near its feet staring up at Cris Mayo.

154

"Damn it!" he said viciously. "You should've been dead! I—!"

"You're a bold lad," Cris said quietly, "and big with your mouth, shootin' at a man from behind the rocks, like."

The man's weapon had fallen a dozen feet off. Cris took his belt-gun from him, then went for the rifle. That made three he had.

"What are you going to do to me?" the man demanded.

Cris shrugged. "I've no use for you, and you've a bullet through your leg that's no help to you, at all. I think I've done enough."

He looked thoughtfully at the chestnut. "It's not often you see a man riding a mare in this country. I think you're the first I've seen."

"That mare's better than any horse you ever saw!"

The fellow was pulling himself into a sitting position, one hand gripping his wounded leg. "You going to leave me here?"

Cris removed his derby. "Right through the crown. That was new when I left Ireland, and now she's ruined. And you figured to put that bullet through my head . . . why shouldn't I leave you?" He glanced at the chestnut. "Still, anybody who owns a horse like that, and keeps it in good shape like that, can't be the worst of men."

Cris looked carefully around. He did not like the place, it was too much like a trap; but the man was hurt, and hurt bad. Also, he had cared for his horse. The mare was in fine condition and showed evidence of the currycomb.

He swung down. "All right, I'll fix you up and take you where you can get a runnin' start. After that, you're a free man till your evil deeds catch up to you."

Cris put his hat on the ground atop his folded coat, then with all arms but his own pistol safely out of reach, he cut away the wounded man's pant-leg.

The bullet had not broken the bone, but apparently glanced from it, tearing a nasty gash. There was little

155

enough he could do, but he built a small fire and heated water in the coffeepot from his saddlebag and bathed the wound, then bound it with a few strips from the wounded man's shirt.

"I'll help you to your horse, man. Then I'll start you off for the trail. If you'll take my advice, you'll be after riding a far piece. There's trouble a-coming for the likes of you! From what they tell me, General Sherman is no mild man, nor are the folks at Laramie."

"I'll ride."

Cris lifted him up, then slipping an arm around the wounded man's waist he helped him to the mare, who stood quietly while he heaved her owner into the saddle.

The fellow looked down at him, a man with a square jaw and a lean, rugged look. He held out his hand. "You'll shake? I'm sorry I shot at you. That's the trouble with this country, a man never knows who he's shooting. I'm Parry Blessing. I rode out of Dundaff in Pennsylvania too long ago, and was living with an uncle in Virginia when the war came on, so I joined up and fought it out, and here I am, a man scarce thirty with a feeling that death is on him. All from bad companions, like they say! And your name?"

"Crispin Mayo, from County Cork. I will ride westward to find a ranch there, it might be in California, and raise horses the like of those in Ireland. And if you're an honest man and come riding that way, the door will stand open to you. But you'll owe me for the hat. I'll not likely find its equal in this country."

Blessing turned the mare and rode away, and Cris looked after him. "Ah, it's a fine mare that! I hope she comes to no harm. One thing!" he shouted suddenly. "One thing more!" Blessing pulled up and waited for Cris. "You've been with them. Do they have a girl now? Do they have Barda McClean?"

"They do not," Blessing turned his mare, "but before long they will have her."

"Where are they camped then? You'll not be going back."

"No." Parry Blessing hesitated. "There's a place in the mountains yonder where a tumbling creek comes down.

You go in by the bluff . . . right there . . . and pass under a leaning pine. You'll know the place by the way the rocks stand, and they'll be there. The major wanted you to use for bait to get the girl out, but he's got another plan in mind now. Tonight or tomorrow at latest he'll take her, right from the fort." He paused. "Robb's with Parley, and Contego, and Murray and some others. And they're wild for revenge."

"My thanks. Be off with you now, and have a care for the mare."

He glanced once, to see the man riding away, and then he started the black for Fort Sanders.

It might be the truth and it might not, but Cris was inclined to believe Blessing. And if they took Barda again, she would not escape them.

Chapter Seventeen

The land lay still under the mounting moon, the night's calm had come to the wild lonely land, and Crispin Mayo, riding toward Fort Sanders, heard no sound but the clop-clop of his horse's hoofs.

A strangeness lay upon him, a feeling of lonely longing for a something nameless . . . was it the night? Was it the land?

A newcomer he was, but the strangeness that lay upon him was not that he was foreign, for he had no longer felt himself a stranger; this land was his and he belonged to it by right of what he had done in this week, and he knew that he would not go back to wherever it was that he had come from. He was not of County Cork any longer, but of the West. The strangeness was only a sense, a vague feeling that he was unable to define or to place.

He rode with guns now, many guns, but the guns no longer reminded him of their presence, for in these days they had become part of him, ready to his hand. Men in this land could own guns, not to threaten their neighbor but to ensure themselves of liberty. The men who shaped this land were men who had lately fought a war for their freedom and they did not wish it to be lost, and so they must keep close to their hands the weapons with which they had won that freedom.

Far off a few lights appeared.

Fort Sanders, Laramie, a few nearby ranches. How warm and welcoming a house light looks to a lonely night-riding man! Someday with luck he would walk into such a house, strike a match, lift the chimney and touch the flame to the wick of his own lamp, sit down in his own house. He would smell the fire smells, the warm cooking smells, and he would stretch out his legs under his table with a faint sigh. He would rest then . . . he would dream, and he would rise from time to time to add a log or to stir the coals in his own fire.

For a time now he had been passing lighted windows, but always in the solitary houses of other men. He slowed his horse. He was near a house and a man was leaving the stable carrying a lantern and a milk pail. He was walking slowly to the house with a small halo of light about his feet, a homely halo, not of heaven this, but of peace, of home.

His door would creak open, it would close behind him, and the night would be dark again, but a resting dark. The man would sit down, relax tired muscles, and reach for a newspaper or a book, or he would talk in low tones to his wife.

"Let us not lose this," Cris muttered aloud, "let us not lose this, God, for there is no greater beauty, no better hour."

He rode into the street of Laramie and to the livery stable, and saw the hostler turn slow eyes to watch him approach. Cris pulled up. "I had the horse from Brennan," he said. "I shall be needing him again."

"I know the horse," the man said, "and you too. I seen you fight."

"He'll need care, and I must be seeing Brennan." Cris stepped down, bundling the rifles together in his arms. "Has there been trouble in town? Are the generals back?"

"There's been no more trouble than always, and the generals is all back, and good hunting it was for them, both buffalo and men."

"And Brennan?"

"That lot came back too, and they had good hunting, I'd say. They brought some bodies, some prisoners, and a few spare horses." Then he added, "And don't tell me when a horse needs care, young fellow. I cared for better horses than this before you'd let go o' the nipple."

"Be seeing to it, then. And as for the nipple, man, why, I was weaned on a jug and a fist."

"I've seen your fists. You handle 'em well, though you got no friend in the conductor. He enjoyed being the top dog around here. He walked with hard heels, that one. And you spoiled it for him."

Crispin Mayo walked across the street. He slapped at his pants to shake the dust loose, and at his coat. He took off his hat and put his fingers through his hair . . . the little finger was still sore as blazes . . . and he looked at the hat.

A fine hat, that one. The best he'd ever owned, and now a bullet hole through the crown. Well, better there than lower. He could always get a new hat.

Brennan was behind the bar. He had a black cigar in his teeth and he looked past it at Cris and then put a beer on the bar. "You'll be needing that, Mayo. It is dry work chasing men."

"Is Barda McClean at the fort?"

"You ask them. They tell me nothing. I'd guess that she is. There's talk of buffalo and renegades there to-night." Brennan nudged the beer closer. "And where have you been? We scoured the country, and thought you were dead in some thicket and the black nag strayed or stolen."

"I was shot, and missed the fight. The black is fine. The worst of the lot are still out there, though I killed a few. I hear that Parley will try to take Barda McClean this night."

"The man's a fool. Does he never know when to quit?"

"I spoke with a man named Parry Blessing, a man riding a lovely mare. He told me they would try."

"Did you kill him?"

"I did not. I tied up his leg that my bullet tore and sent him off. I had a powerful longing for the mare and was afraid that if I shot him it would be for her, so I let him ride off."

"She's a fine one, well-behaved and a runner and jumper. I've tried to buy her, thought of stealing her, and tried to win her from him gambling . . . he would not bet the mare. His gun, his shirt, even his saddle, but not the mare." Brennan shook his head in grudging admiration.

"I'll be riding to the fort. I must speak with the colonel."

Cris finished his beer. He was tired, dead tired. That did not begin to describe his feelings. He was dead-and-buried tired. And yet as he turned away from the bar he could think only of his reception at the fort.

They would doubt his statement, of course. Taking someone right out of a fort with soldiers around seemed absurd. Parley, though, was just the madman to attempt such a thing, and Del Robb would go along, and likely Murray.

Brennan spoke behind him. "Cris, there's hard feeling in town. The people here want no more of this, and we've had several sluggings on the street. There's much cheating and too much gunplay. They're getting tired of it. And Sam Calkins still has nasty friends. Be careful of yourself."

"Me?" He was startled.

"You're a stranger to some of them, others know you only as a prizefighter. When a mob starts a cleanup and you're caught in the wrong place . . . well, mistakes can be made."

Cris nodded. Then he saw his three rifles, where he'd leaned them against the bar. "Here," he said, "you may as well have two of these, Owen Brennan. I have no use for more than one, and you have been a fair man and generous to me."

"Bring them down to the end of the bar," said Brennan. Cris gathered them up; their weight seemed to have doubled, he was so weary. He carried them down the tent saloon to where Brennan had pointed.

"You took them off Parley's men?"

"Men I had occasion to knock down, yes."

"I'll pay you for them, they're good weapons." Brennan ran a practiced eye over the rifles. "You keep that one, Mayo, that's the best. Lean this way." Shielded by both their bodies, he slipped a heavy leather bag inside Cris' inside coat pocket. "You'll find the thousand that

I promised you in that, and a little besides to cover the guns."

Cris considered. "Brennan, you're a credit to Donegal, and I thank you. Would you do me one favor? Keep it for me till I've seen this business through? I am so tired," he said frankly, "that I dread the weight of all that metal. It might lay me in the gutter."

Brennan uttered a hard bark of amusement. "Mayo, I'm thinking it would take a herd of buffalo to lay you in the gutter."

"No," said Cris, "I've stood one of their charges already. But Parley's men might do it. If I don't come back, give this to Reppato Pratt, who's a decent fellow." He handed the sack over, picked up his rifle, and walked outside. The air was cool. Autumn was here, and the nights were growing colder.

Brennan followed him to the door. "You'll be wanting to rest the black. Ask George for the buckskin with the Slash-4-C brand."

George looked up at him with hooded eyes. "You again? Don't you ever sleep?"

"I want the buckskin."

"I heard him through the wall." George got up. "You're dead on your feet. Want to crawl into the hay back yonder?"

"After. I'm riding up to the fort." He looked at George. "Keep your eyes about you. Some of the Parley outfit may be sneaking in tonight."

"They won't come here." George threw the saddle on the buckskin and cinched up, punching the horse in the belly to make him let the wind out. "You know Hazel Kerry? She's got a shack over back o' here. She's friendly to some of them. Especially to Del . . . you know, the gunman."

Cris pulled himself into the saddle, scabbarding his rifle. "I may make a call when I get back. I am getting sick of this."

He was challenged at the gate. The sentry held him for the corporal of the guard, who turned out to be Halloran. He chuckled as he showed Cris his new

162

stripes. "Ordered by Sherman himself, just before they left the fort."

"They're gone?"

"The generals are. Colonel McClean is still here. He's going on west in the morning, with his daughter."

"I must see him."

Halloran glanced toward the officers' quarters. "They've gone to bed, Cris. You will have to wait until tomorrow."

Cris explained, fumbling a little with the words. All he wanted to do was just lie down and sleep for a week, and he did not care where it was, any bed, any barn, anywhere.

Halloran was dubious. "All right," he said at last. "I'll walk over with you. If there's a shred of light, I'll chance waking them."

The parade ground was dark and empty. They walked across, not talking. Crispin Mayo's eyes felt hot and tired, and various portions of his anatomy screamed for ointments and bandages. He was in no very pleasant mood, and wanted only to have it done with, all of it.

There was light in a window, and Halloran knocked. After a moment, McClean himself opened the door, a pistol in his hand. "You, is it, youngster? What's the trouble?"

"It's still Parley, sir. I talked with one of his men. They've an idea to take your daughter again. Strictly revenge this time, I think."

"The man's insane."

"He is, sir. But that's the trouble. He *will* try it. I talked with him also. . . . He sees himself as a last hero of the South, not as the renegade and outlaw that he is. He'll try it, Colonel."

Barda had appeared behind her father. Her hair was down around her shoulders and she wore a robe over her nightgown. Cris removed his hat.

"Father? Let Mr. Mayo sleep here. Can't you see? He's so tired and beaten that he can scarcely stand."

Colonel McClean looked sharply at him, then smiled. "All right, we're crowded, but I'll have a bed made for you on the sofa. Come in, Mayo. We do owe you far more than a bed."

He stepped out on the porch and gave orders to Halloran for a heavier guard to be posted.

When he came back into the room, Barda herself was there with blankets, covering the sofa. Cris had put his hat on the table and removed his coat. He was ashamed at the condition of his clothes. "I've been riding," he said apologetically. "I've had no time to change."

Barda turned to say something to him, and gave a cry of horror. "Cris, you've been wounded! Your side!"

"It's nothing at all," he said, embarrassed, "only a slight flesh wound."

"How do you know? I'll bet you haven't even looked at it," she snapped. "Take off your shirt."

"With your permission, miss, I will not. It's not fitting, and you the daughter of a great officer and being a well-bred young lady and all."

"Cris, I'm going to cleanse that wound." She was opening a chest, dragging out linens, bandages, medicine bottles. "Don't worry, I've doctored before," she said, "I'm an Army brat."

"She's right, Cris," put in the colonel, "you do need some looking after."

"A good night's sleep," said Cris desperately, "that's all I need to set me as right as—"

"Cris Mayo, you do as I say!" said Barda McClean.

"But it is not seemly!"

"Bother *seemly*! Bother *fitting*! Take off that shirt!" she shouted.

"Yes, Miss McClean," said Cris humbly. He peeled it off, wincing as the hard-clotted blood tore loose from the wound. He sat on the edge of the sofa and submitted to some twenty minutes of cleansing, dabbing, anointing and wrapping. His head was gone over thoroughly by the two of them, the colonel pressing here and there with expert fingers.

"You had a bad fall, I think."

"A couple of them, yes sir."

"You're lucky you don't have a fractured skull. I

164

think you're going to be all right. Barda, put a bandage on that finger, my dear. I believe you received the cut eye in the match yesterday? It's healing nicely. Mayo, you've taken a deal of punishment lately."

"Trouble keeps turnin' up in me path, sir, it seems."

Barda said, "Lie down and rest, Cris, I'll get you a cup of tea."

"Now that would be grand. I've had no real tea since I left Ireland, and a cup of it would warm me nicely."

Barda went to the kitchen. Cris tugged off his boots, and after some protesting, accepted one of the colonel's own shirts to replace his ruined one. Then he stretched out with a sigh. He was tired. He'd never been so tired in his—

Barda came in and stopped, teacup in hand. Mc-Clean was smiling. "He's asleep. Don't worry about the tea. I will drink it myself."

He picked up the hat and stared at the bullet hole. "Close," he said, "very close indeed." McClean looked down at Cris, who was dead to the world around him. "That's quite a man, honey. Quite a man. And you were right . . . he is a natural gentleman."

Chapter Eighteen

Dawn fingered the curtains with light, and Cris opened his eyes. The room was shadowed and quiet, totally unfamiliar.

It came to him suddenly. Colonel McClean's quarters at Fort Sanders. He sat up. There'd been no attempt then, during the night. And the Colonel and Barda were to leave today . . . that meant the attack would come today. It would be today for certain.

He swung his feet to the floor and got his boots on, then his hat. He had slept with his gun in its holster. He took it out and spun the cylinder . . . fully loaded.

He checked the belt-loops: fourteen cartridges left. It should be enough, for his rifle was loaded and he had a few more rounds for it in his coat.

Taking up his hat, he tiptoed to the door, then thought of what he was doing and returned. On the table was an envelope and a bit of pencil. He wrote on it, *Thank you. If I can make it I will go to the train.*

He tiptoed outside, put on his hat, and started across the parade ground at the very moment when the troops were falling out. Halloran was there. "I'll need my horse," said Cris.

"You're leaving early. What happened?"

"I remembered a thing that the hostler told me. He said that some of the Parley crowd are friendly with a woman named Hazel Kerry. If they haven't tried anything by now, they will try at the station or on the train. I'm going down to see her."

He flexed his fingers. They felt good, and so did he, amazingly good. He mounted the buckskin and rode out of the gate at a canter.

166

His rifle was in its scabbard. He drew the pistol, liking the way it slid so easily into his hand. He had always been skillful with his hands. He tried drawing the gun as he rode, and it came easily, smoothly. He was no fast-draw expert, but it handled well enough.

Make the first shot count, they said. All right, that was what he would do. No more wild firing out of impatience, from now on. No more banging away to frighten people.

He left the horse at the stable. George came out of his room, slipping his suspenders over his shoulders. "You again. What now?"

"I shall pay a visit. I want to see if that woman, Hazel Kerry, is entertaining guests."

"Be careful. That's a bad lot. Oh, I don't mean Hazel! She ain't no worse than any of 'em, and better than some. It's just that Del taken a fancy to her."

Cris hesitated, then left the rifle. In close quarters it might not be so handy, and he was hoping there would be no shooting, anyway.

He followed George's pointing finger. "See? The little white house back of Cooney's corral. You can't miss it."

The sun was not yet over the horizon, but the gray early light of morning lay on the town. Somewhere a door slammed, a rooster crowed, and a pail jangled. He walked out of the back of the barn, crawled through the livery-stable fence and strode up the alley.

There were several horses in Cooney's corral, but he recognized none of them. He stopped at the corner of the corral, looking past it at the white house.

Small . . . yet there'd be three, probably four rooms. He'd best go to the back door.

The curtains were drawn, no lights showed. His hand went to the holster and loosened the gun slightly. He did not want it to bind in the leather just when he needed it.

Crispin Mayo, of County Cork and Wyoming Territory, looked across the thirty feet that separated him from the house. He hoped they would not see him as he crossed that last short stretch of ground.

He hesitated, took a long breath, and started out. A rock rolled under his foot, clicking against another. A puff of dust arose. Suddenly he was at the back stoop. The steps creaked, and he knocked lightly.

There was a moment of silence, then the door opened so softly that he knew she was trying to make no sound. A girl stood framed in the door, a girl with red hair curling softly around her face. It had been done up but it was falling now, and despite the hardness around the eyes and the lips she was beautiful. And he knew her.

"I am asking for Hazel Kerry," he said.

"That is what they call me," she said quietly. "Hello, Crispin, and a good morning to you."

"Invite him in," a voice suggested, "since you seem to know him so well."

She hesitated. "Go away, Crispin. Go away quickly now, and if you get back to County Cork, do me a kindness and say nothing of this, or of me."

"I'll not speak of it, and well you know that," Cris replied, "but the gentleman wished to see me."

He stepped in as she moved back. Del Robb was there, a darkly handsome man with a taunting smile. "So you know each other? You didn't tell me, darlin'."

"She did not know I was about," Cris said quietly. "It is a far piece from here to where we met, and that in passing only. It was at a county fair one time . . . in Ireland."

"Ah? Well, I'm glad you could get together again, if only for a minute or two."

"She is going west, I think," Cris chose his words carefully. "From what is said, there'll soon be no place in town for any on the wrong side of the law. There is trouble coming."

"We like trouble, don't we, darlin'?" Robb smiled. "And you, Irish boy, are you huntin' trouble? It seems to me that every time I turn around your name's coming up. I think we ought to end all that."

"You too," Cris said quietly, "you, Parley and the rest of them. The war you fought is over, and it does no good to carry it on and make trouble for your people."

The kitchen was bright with newborn sunlight now. It was clean and neat, the kitchen of one who liked keeping it so.

"There'll be another house, in another town, Hazel Kerry," he said quietly. "Do yourself a favor and take the westbound train. There'll be shooting and burning now, from what they're saying, and it will be no good place for a woman alone."

"When any shooting's done, I'll do it," Robb said.

"Against vigilantes? They will hang you, Robb, if you're in town."

"I've heard such talk before! It's only balderdash!"

"Is it now? The murmur of their planning is all about, and you'll find they know where all of you are, and they've the places chosen and the ropes knotted. You'd be wise to ride now, ride far and fast."

"Don't be a fool." Robb's laugh was jeering. "No shanty Irishman's going to frighten me off with stories. And if I do go," he smiled, "I'll have your scalp at my belt."

"In front of the lady?" Cris said. "You'd kill a man in front of a lady?"

"A lady? *Her?*" He brayed again.

The man was going to kill him. Cris knew that was Robb's intent. He was showing off a bit like the bully he was, and then he was going to try.

"I am no gunfighter," Cris said, "my way is with the fists."

"Not this time, Irish. I'm going to kill you when I—"

Crispin Mayo had no hope of beating him, but he needed the extra split second and he drew first. His big hand was only inches from the gun and it swung back, closed on the butt, his finger touched the trigger and the gun swung up.

Del Robb had been confident and contemptuous. He knew Cris Mayo had used a gun but little, being fresh from a country where they did not carry guns, and he had expected him to back off, to beg, to fumble for the weapon at least. He did none of these, nor was he clumsy. The split second of reaction time was enough.

Robb's move was late, hurried. Mentally he was caught off balance, and the distance was less than ten feet.

Robb's gun was coming up when the bullet hit him. He felt the sharp, hard nudge in the midsection and his fist closed convulsively on the gun. The bullet plowed a groove in the floor and Del Robb lifted on his toes, then dropped back on his heels, his gun still coming up, his eyes hot with fury.

Crispin Mayo was a fighting man, and his way was to step in, to follow up with his punches, and so he stepped in now. Two quick steps even as his bullet struck and then he thumbed the hammer twice more, rapid-fire, at a range of four feet.

Robb's eyes opened very wide and he backed up to the door jamb and leaned there. "You lucky son-of-a—!"

Cris slapped the gun from his hand with a blow. It fell to the floor, and Robb still stood, leaning against the door jamb, his knees slowly weakening. Then he toppled onto his face.

Cris stepped back, turning to Hazel Kerry. "I am sorry," he said.

"Save it for somebody who needs it," she said. "I never liked him. I was afraid of him. He threatened me."

"Forget this," Cris waved a hand around him. "Pack what you can and catch that train. You've got about an hour, but please . . . don't miss it!"

He thumbed cartridges into the gun, then holstered it. "Where are the others? Do you know?"

"That's the trouble, I don't know! Only that they are here, in town."

"Get on the train. Don't wait until the last minute, just go down there now."

He went outside into the full glare of the sun. Reppato Pratt and Halloran were coming toward him from the stable.

"What happened?" Rep asked, stopping him.

"The rest of them are here. We've got to find them."

"Don't worry," Halloran said, "the McCleans are coming through town with a troop of cavalry. They'll be put on the train that way, and a squad will stay with them all the way to the end of track and then accompany their stage to California. General Sherman's orders."

170

"Who was in there? I mean, besides Hazel?" Rep asked.

"Del Robb. He's dead."

They stared at him, scarcely believing, yet knowing that he would not joke at such a time. *Del Robb!*

He walked across to the saloon. Down the street at Brennan's *Belle of the West* several men were standing. Their horses were at the rail, dusty and hard-ridden. Cris went inside and Brennan took his cigar from his teeth. "I have your money for you, Mayo, if you're strong enough to carry it now." He counted it out on the bar in gold pieces, then replaced it in the bag. "Take it, lad. You're going on with McClean?"

"To California, I think. I want to start a horse ranch."

"So you said. Well, you've got a mare waiting for you at the station. It's Parry Blessing's mare. He sent it to you, as a gift."

Cris shook his head. "That can't be true. He'll never give that horse up while he lives."

"That's just it. He's dead . . . killed by one of the Parley crowd, but with his last breath he said he wanted you to have the mare, so somebody brought it in."

"That's a fine mare." Crispin Mayo considered the situation. "You say somebody brought her in. Who?"

"We don't know who they are. Some strangers who got to Blessing before he died. Interrupted Parley's killer before he could steal her. They left the mare at the hitching rail down by the station."

Cris rested his big hands on the edge of the bar. He considered the subject. Then he said, "Brennan, I want to buy you a drink. And one for each of these gentlemen. I will have a beer."

"I never touch the stuff," Brennan said, "but I'll take a cigar. Luck to you."

"Blessing knew I had eyes for that horse," Cris said, a little sadly. "I'll be glad to have her. But I'm sorry for him. We could have been friends."

Far away they heard the train whistle. Cris tasted the beer. "Come with me, Rep. I'll need help, and nobody knows mustang horses better than you."

171

"Cris, I think I just might do that. 'Cause you're dead right about that."

"Troopers coming," Brennan said. "That means McClean and his daughter."

Crispin Mayo drank his beer, drank again, and put down the glass. He held out a hand. "You'll be coming on west, Brennan. Once the railroad's built through, there'll be naught to keep you here."

"I might at that." Brennan shook, and nipped the end from his cigar. "Cris, keep your gun handy."

They went outside onto the boardwalk. Cris Mayo went to the stable, retrieved his rifle, and with his two friends walked along down the street toward the tracks. He remembered his carpetbag at the hotel. Let it stay, there was nothing in it but shabby clothes. The train whistled again. "I'll be able to load the mare with McClean's horses," he said aloud. "There'll be room enough."

They passed men, talking quietly in small groups; they glanced at Rep, then at Cris, and one made some comment. Several of them turned to look.

A row of buildings faced toward the station. Cris walked past them and crossed the street. The station seemed to be empty. Several idlers loafed about, awaiting the train. Some carpetbags stood where the owners had put them down. A lone man, in a gray suit of English cut, was lighting a pipe, his back toward them.

Rep nodded to indicate the end of the hitching rail. "There's your mare, and a purty sight. Shall we get 'er?"

"Wait." Cris was unsure why he wished to wait, but something warned him that if Parley meant to move it must be now or never.

Two troopers came down the street leading the Colonel's gelding and Barda's mare. Then he saw a rank of riders, a lieutenant beside Colonel McClean, Barda on the other side, ahead of a troop of cavalry.

The two troopers who had brought the horses tied them, then turned to face the oncoming troop. Both men were armed and ready, watching for any overt move.

Halloran, who was off duty, stepped to one side. He was also armed. Rep whispered to Cris, "I don't like this here. Parley'll have sumthin' up his sleeve."

The train whistled again, and they saw it appear far down the track. McClean, the lieutenant and Barda rode to the hitching rail and dismounted. One of the waiting troopers took their horses, which were Army mounts; the gelding and mare were not saddled, but ready to be loaded for their long trip.

Cris walked toward them. "Sir?"

McClean stopped. "How are you today, Mayo? What can I do for you?"

"I have a mare, sir. A very good one that I've inherited. I am going on to California, too, and I wondered if there'd be room enough in the car with your horses? I could pay, sir."

"Of course, and certainly there's no need for you to pay. Sergeant, see to it, will you?" McClean glanced around. "Where is the mare?"

Cris pointed and the sergeant turned toward her. "Wait, Sergeant," Cris spoke quietly, "you'd better let me go. It may be a trap. I believe Parley's men know that I wanted that mare."

The sergeant flipped open the flap on his holster. "Right, sir. I'd like a chance at them."

"It is my mare. You can cover me, if you like." He glanced around. The colonel and Barda were walking slowly toward the train, the lieutenant with them.

Cris turned suddenly, and Rep stepped back quickly to keep from being bumped. "Sergeant! They've got to be aboard this train. The renegades, I mean! It's the only place they can be!"

The sergeant shot a quick, sharp look. "I doubt it, but you could be right." He strolled over to the other troopers, who were dismounting. He spoke, and two of them wheeled their horses and trotted toward the train.

Cris untied the mare and turned toward the ramp that had been lowered from the stockcar. A trooper was already leading the McClean horses toward it. Cris followed. Walking with the mare between himself and the

173

train, he took the moment to draw his gun and push it into his waistband a little closer to his hand.

He watched the horses go up the ramp. He noticed that the engineer had not gotten down from the engine. A brakeman stood by the car where the colonel would ride. He had stepped aside for them to board.

The two troopers had ridden the length of the train, peering in at the windows. They shook their heads.

"Nothing," the sergeant said. "You've overrated them, Mayo."

Cris let his eyes run along the train. Two passenger, cars, the stockcar for the horses, two freight cars, the mail car. Where? *Where?*

He walked down and watched Rep tying the mare in her stall. The car was not a regular stockcar but was fitted with stalls for several horses, and usually used to carry animals belonging to railroad engineers or Army officers. The stalls had been knocked together quite hurriedly.

He looked toward the engine. Nobody in sight. He felt hollow inside and his lips were dry. He could feel deadly danger all about him. His nape crawled with it.

He put his hand in the front of his coat and took hold of his gun, then walked slowly along the cars. The freight car nearest the engine was not sealed. He walked on past it, then stepped over to the sergeant.

"They're in there, I'd stake me life on it! And there's somebody on the tender or hidden in the cab who has a gun on the engineer. Look at him, man! Not even down here to stretch his legs!"

"Not much of a place to hide in that cab," the sergeant was doubtful. "I'll speak to the lieutenant."

He strolled away without haste toward the rear of the train, and Cris watched the freight-car door. They must have some place from which to watch: a crack in the door? At the door's edge?

Suddenly, the whistle blew. The train stirred, started to move. Cris glanced down along the train. McClean and Barda had disappeared into their car.

The sergeant was talking excitedly now to the lieutenant, and the train started to move. Cris knew instantly that the order had been given to pull out, and fast. He turned sharply and grabbed a ladder on the end of the car nearest him, pulling himself up.

Rep, who had descended from the stockcar, jumped for another one and made it.

The lieutenant suddenly started forward, but the train was already moving and he had twenty steps to get to the last car. By the time he reached it the train would be rolling too fast, for it was pulling out at a rapid clip. He *might* order the troop to pursue it, but would probably balk at assuming that much authority on the mere suspicions of an Irish gandy dancer—he'd more likely shrug it off as an idiosyncrasy of the engineer, pulling out fast to make up time. But a squad was supposed to accompany the McCleans! Surely he'd order them, at least, to chase after the train?

Cris climbed to the end of the car next to the suspected one, and sat down near the brake wheel. How could the enemy get out while the train was moving? Or were there horses waiting somewhere ahead, where they planned to stop? Some place where they could ride at once into the Medicine Bow Mountains?

There were doors on either side, but getting out would not be easy while the train moved, unless there was a steep grade like that on which they had originally planned to attack the train, near the little red station where he'd first found himself involved in this devil's dance.

He knew nothing about the grade ahead of them, but Parley would have had it scouted.

There was something else. In the far end of the car there was a small door, large enough for a man to crawl through. Emerging there, they could come down the walk atop the cars to where McClean and Barda were.

He stood up. Walking atop cars was no problem for one so accustomed to the unsteadiness of a ship's deck. He rolled along the catwalk toward the rear of the train and passed over the second freight car. He glanced back once . . . no pursuit so far.

To pull the pin and disconnect the cars would be no

175

advantage, as the freight car in which he believed the outlaws to be was connected to the engine, which would simply back up and make the connection again.

He went down the ladder and entered the car where McClean was. Rep was standing near the colonel. Barda was seated beside him, her face strained, her eyes very large. Only two soldiers had made the train, two of the squad who were supposed to be riding as a guard.

"She pulled out too fast," Rep said tensely. "They were all comin' up to board, but that there engineer, he really taken off. Suthin's wrong."

"Sir," Cris said to McClean, "I believe the enemy are in the car next to the engine. They either plan to come out of the small door in the end of the car nearest the tender, and then back along the catwalk, or else they have horses waiting for them somewhere ahead."

"The engineer?"

"They have him, sir. I know it. He never came down at all. . . . I mean, they must have a man or two riding the front end of the tender, and they've got the drop on the engineer. He does what they say or he gets a bullet in the back."

"I see." McClean glanced around. "That's an intelligent theory. Well, there are at least five of us here who are armed." He stood up and faced the other passengers. There were three men and two women. He raised his voice. "Are any of you men armed?"

A long, lean old man with steel-cold eyes looked up. "Cunnel, I never seen the time sinct I was knee-high to a toad-frog when I didn't carry a shootin' iron."

McClean explained briefly, and the old man spat into a brass spittoon. "I'm headed for Californy, an' I done paid m' fare. I figure to go right through on this hyar train to Hell-on-Wheels and then on the stage, an' nobody ain't goin' to mess up m' ride. Sinct I was a boy I been aimin' to ride these steam-cyars. If them fellers are fixin' to worry us, or to cause trouble for the purty young lady, you count on me. I figure to fetch one or two of 'em."

Rep looked at Cris and grinned. There was an ally worth having.

McClean turned to the others. One, a fat-cheeked drummer with a pearl-gray derby, pulled a six-shooter from under his coat and waved it. "Yessir. I'll be standin' by."

A buxom blonde with a tightly cinched waist took a .44 Remington from her valise. She laid it in her lap and smiled up at them. "The soldier boys always stood by me when there was trouble, so you can deal the cards, Colonel. I'll play them like you say."

"My compliments, ma'am," said McClean, bowing.

The third man stood up. He was the man in the English-cut suit and his face was flushed. "You think there will be shooting?"

"I hope not," McClean replied, "but it does look possible."

"I have a shotgun," the dude suggested. "I brought it out hoping to try it on prairie chickens or quail, but if you think—"

"When the time comes," McClean suggested, "just point it at them and squeeze off your shots. You'll get some birds, all right, some very tough birds!"

The second woman was Hazel Kerry. Without speaking, she showed them a pearl-handled derringer.

"Mayo, my lad," said Colonel McClean almost gaily, "it's a regular army we have here! Ten guns! Parley can't have figured on that!"

Cris laid his rifle on a seat and checked his pistol again. The train rumbled over a trestle, then curved through a cut in the hills and emerged into open country. Up ahead the whistle blew . . . now what was that for?

He peered from the window, squinting his eyes against the cinders and the blown smoke. The smell of coal smoke was thick in his nostrils. He could see nothing moving up ahead; the country was rugged with much brown grass, many thrust-up rocks. The train whistled again, a long, drawn-out whistle that sounded lonesomely across the hills. The train rumbled over another trestle, and he shifted his feet restlessly.

"I am going up there," he said to McClean. "I think that was a signal. Maybe I can keep them bottled up."

He started for the end of the car and Rep and the old man followed him.

"If they got the ingin," the old man said happily, "mebbe we can dust 'em out o' there."

Cris led the way, stepping from the front of the car to the coupling, then, catching hold of the ladder on the next car, he climbed up. He walked along the swaying catwalk, stepped over space to the next car, and suddenly a man raised up on the tender holding a Winchester. The fellow took his stance and lifted the rifle to his shoulder.

From behind him Cris heard the ugly crash of a gun, and the man with the rifle took a slow step backward atop the coal, sat down, and then did a somersault and vanished.

The train whistled again, and began to slow down. Cris moved forward again along the swaying top of the car.

Out of the hills to the left came a small group of riders and eight or nine led horses.

Cris jumped to the tender. He saw the body of the man who had been shot and a second man raising up, turning toward him. Unwilling to risk shooting the engineer, Cris shoved his gun into his holster and leaped.

The man tried to step back and Cris' shoulder hit him in the chest. The man went backwards down the steps and Cris, unable to check himself, plunged after him, hit the ground atop him, and rolled over with him while the train went racing on.

As it swept by, Cris heard the passengers shooting from the coach, a barking, roaring volley; and when he staggered to his feet, momentarily groggy from the fall, he saw the horses rearing and plunging and a couple of the riders in full flight toward the mountains.

He turned sharply to stare at the man who had fallen ahead of him. The fellow lay on the ground, all sprawled out, his head cocked at an impossible angle. Cris stripped the body of its six-gun and slung the belt about his own waist. Then the body rolled over and groaned, feeling for its neck. Cris could have sworn that neck had been broken.

The train was disappearing in the distance.

He was alone, and somewhere across the tracks were the outlaws and their horses. The first thing was to get out of sight.

The train might come back for him. Yet no sooner had the thought occurred than he dismissed it. Not with a carload of renegades waiting to strike, and all of them aware that their plan had again gone wrong.

He glanced quickly around, then ran for the nearest rocks. It was a nest of boulders, but offered little in the way of shelter. Using it to conceal his movements from the sight of the outlaw he had left behind on the ground, he ran on toward a similar group of stones.

Here were a few low trees and surprisingly enough, a ravine. He went down into it and hiked along, heading for higher ground. Cris had no idea of leaving the railroad where lay his one chance for help, but merely wished to be away when the enemy returned . . . if they did.

He found a crack in the rocks and climbed inside it to the top, where he lay down in the brown grass and peered out over the country below.

The outlaw was on his feet, looking around. How conscious had he been? Would he remember that somebody else had fallen with him? Or assume that he was alone?

The man felt at his waist . . . his gun and belt were gone.

That would give him away, Cris thought. But he had needed the cartridges.

The outlaw started across the tracks, found the prints of the horses, and stood there, hands on hips, probably swearing. Cris Mayo was too far off to hear any words, but he knew the attitude. Soon the man started off, following the tracks of the horses. From time to time he paused and looked around carefully.

Cris Mayo settled his square-cut derby on his head and watched the outlaw. The fellow would try to track down his friends, but he'd better hurry or they would be gone. After the failure of this final attempt there would

179

certainly be no more, and it was likely that within a short time the whole lot would be prisoners.

Yet his own situation was desperate. He was alone, without a horse, and in wild country. He was a long way from Fort Sanders, and perhaps even farther from the next station to the west.

From his vantage point he began to examine the country along the tracks. He was well up on the side of a hill, and in such a position that his view extended for miles.

Removing his coat with its heavy sack of coins, he slung it over his shoulder and plodded down the hillside to the tracks.

There was nothing for it but to follow them.

The sun was hot. He walked steadily, avoiding the unevenly spaced ties. He removed his collar and thrust it into his coat pocket, and, folding his tie, did the same with it. His eyes swept the country. They were much better eyes now than they had ever been, more accustomed to looking at the wide western lands and selecting what was important. He mopped his brow and marched forward.

He was carrying two pistols, the one "inherited" from the dead telegrapher and the one taken from the unconscious outlaw. He had ammunition enough but it was heavy, as the guns were heavy. From time to time he paused, swiped at the sweat on his face, looked all around, then started on.

He was thirsty, but there was no water. The earth was a powdery dust studded with sagebrush wherever his eyes went.

The sun was past the nooning by more than two hours when he saw the cabin. It was built of native stone and it stood back from the right-of-way beside what seemed to be an old road. When he got closer he could see the remains of a pole corral.

He put his ear down on a steel rail to listen for a train, but heard nothing. Seated on the railroad embankment, he gazed toward the stone cabin. It looked innocent enough, and there was a touch of green behind it . . . perhaps there was a spring.

He rested, watching the cabin. He checked the pistol taken from the outlaw . . . it was loaded with five cartridges.

He returned it to the holster, which was on his left hip with the butt facing forward. When he carried his coat over his left arm this gun was concealed, while his right-hand gun was fully in sight.

The stone cabin was probably empty, and there was a chance of water. It was unlikely that anybody would have built here without it, and the green seemed an indication. He got to his feet, the coat over his left forearm, the second gun hidden behind it.

Cris plodded on. His feet were sore and he was tired. Some of yesterday's pains had awakened to plague him. He looked along the tracks, and saw nothing. In the distance he glimpsed a small herd of antelope. He kept his face turned down the track but from the corners of his eyes he watched the cabin for movement.

This was Indian country, but there were outlaws around too, and they might be anywhere.

Opposite the cabin he halted, then turned down a dim path that led from the right-of-way to the door. Still he saw no movement there.

The door sagged on leather hinges, one window gaped emptily at him. He walked around the cabin and followed a path evidently used by men as well as animals to a few willows and a small cottonwood. The latter grew in a slight hollow and was invisible from the track. At its base was a ring of rocks forming a tank, and the tank was filled with clear water, which trickled from a pipe above it.

He bent his head and drank, waited, then drank again. The water was cold, a little brackish but good. He straightened up and glancing down saw some crushed shells under his feet. Idly, he stooped to pick one up and as his fingers touched it he saw a fresh boot track, in which a blade of grass was just springing erect.

Slowly, his heart pounding, he straightened up. Whoever had made that track was close by, within yards of him, no doubt.

A sharply cut boot track . . . no moccasin.

He appeared to be studying the shell, while his mind raced. The path he followed had gone on from the tank, dimmer, but still there. Willows stood on the far side of the tank, and there was something behind them . . . a dugout or a cave, he believed, where horses had been kept.

"Well, now!" He knew the voice. "What could be purtier than this? You come walkin' right up to me, just like you'd been sent for!"

He stared to turn, and the voice hardened. "Hold it!" It was Murray. Murray, who had been after Barda, and who had been given a beating by Cris. Murray, who wanted and intended to kill him.

"Now you take hold of the butt of that six-shooter, just thumb and finger now! You lift it clear and drop it. Then you can turn around. I want you to see me and this here gun. I want the last sight you have to be *me*, standing here shootin' you down!"

"Can't we talk about this?" Gently, careful to make no mistake, he lifted the gun and dropped it. It thudded on the earth.

"Now you step back one good step . . . that's it. Now you can turn around."

Murray would have a gun held steady on him, Cris was sure. Murray was set to kill him, and Murray wanted him to see it coming. And Murray would not talk long before he shot . . . he was too full of hate.

Crispin Mayo knew that the movement might be his last, but he turned his left shoulder and side toward Murray and as he did so his right hand came up under cover of the movement and the coat. The six-gun slid easily into his hand, rested on his forearm.

The time for talking, for thinking, for mercy, was past. The gun cleared his arm, and his finger closed easy on the trigger, the barrel pointed straight at Murray.

The first thing Murray could have seen was the blossom of flame at the gun's muzzle, and it was almost the last thing.

His own six-shooter dropped from fingers gone suddenly dead, and Murray went to his knees. "You damn Irish tenderfoot! You—!"

"I am no tenderfoot, Mr. Murray. Not any longer."

Murray sagged back, half-falling over. "I guess you ain't," he muttered. "Damn you, Irish! I shoulda left you alone! Your medicine's bad for me, you—" Then he crumpled.

Crispin Mayo, of County Cork and the great plains of the West, stood watching him for several minutes. The man was dead.

Picking up the gun he had been forced to drop, he wiped the dirt away and then walked back into the willows. Murray's dapple gray horse was there, with a freshly filled canteen on the saddle. He led the beast outside, let it water again, and then swung into the saddle and rode down the trail to the railroad.

He was there beside the track when he heard the train whistle, no more than a minute later. He stepped down, removed the canteen, then held the reins until he saw that the train was slowing down for him. He threw the reins over the saddle and slapped the horse on the hip. "You've got a home somewhere. Go!"

When the train stopped and a conductor stepped down, it was Sam Calkins. A dozen soldiers peered from the windows.

"You'd better get aboard," Calkins said sourly, "Colonel McClean and his daughter are waitin' for you at Medicine Bow."

Crispin Mayo climbed into the car, lifted a hand to the soldiers and dropped into a seat.

"Thought I heard shootin'." Calkins was reluctantly curious. "We were comin' along slow, had no idea where you'd be."

Cris opened his eyes. "Murray was up there at the spring. That was his horse I turned loose."

He closed his eyes again. He had no idea how far it was to Medicine Bow.

Barda would be there—

Cris Mayo slept without dreams.

The train whistle called again, losing itself against the silent hills, calling to the empty ghosts that watched there wide-eyed. The drivers threshed at the rails, and the train started along the track. Again the whistle called, and the sound seemed to hang in the stillness.

The following night, Justin Parley, aware that ten of his men had been taken from the train in Medicine Bow and the rest killed or scattered, rode boldly into Laramie. At the edge of the town Silver Dick suddenly pulled up. "Major," he said, "I cached some coin about a month ago, right back there by the barn. You go ahead. I'll join you at the *Belle*."

"Of course," Parley said, and rode on alone. Silver Dick Contego paused on the hill. "Good-bye, Justin," he said quietly. "You believe in your star, I believe in a fast horse."

The night was cool, clear, splendid to see. Tonight was the 29th of October, 1868, a date never to be forgotten in Fort Sanders and Laramie. It was the night when the vigilantes cleaned up the town, concentrating their energies on the *Belle of the West*. Five men were killed, many were wounded, a good deal of lead was thrown; and Justin Parley, who never used his own name in Laramie, was dropped next morning into an unmarked grave.

ABOUT THE AUTHOR

LOUIS L'AMOUR, born Louis Dearborn L'Amour, is of French-Irish descent. Although Mr. L'Amour claims his writing began as a "spur-of-the-moment thing," prompted by friends who relished his verbal tales of the West, he comes by his talent honestly. A frontiersman by heritage (his grandfather was scalped by the Sioux), and a universal man by experience, Louis L'Amour lives the life of his fictional heroes. Since leaving his native Jamestown, North Dakota, at the age of fifteen, he's been a longshoreman, lumberjack, elephant handler, hay shocker, flume builder, fruit picker, and an officer on tank destroyers during World War II. And he's written four hundred short stories and over fifty books (including a volume of poetry).

Mr. L'Amour has lectured widely, traveled the West thoroughly, studied archaeology, compiled biographies of over one thousand Western gunfighters, and read prodigiously (his library holds more than two thousand volumes). And he's watched thirty-one of his westerns as movies. He's circled the world on a freighter, mined in the West, sailed a dhow on the Red Sea, been shipwrecked in the West Indies, stranded in the Mojave Desert. He's won fifty-one of fifty-nine fights as a professional boxer and pinch-hit for Dorothy Kilgallen when she was on vacation from her column. Since 1816, thirty-three members of his family have been writers. And, he says, "I could sit in the middle of Sunset Boulevard and write with my typewriter on my knees; temperamental I am not."

Mr. L'Amour is re-creating an 1865 Western town, christened Shalako, where the borders of Utah, Arizona, New Mexico, and Colorado meet. Historically authentic from whistle to well, it will be a live, operating town, as well as a movie location and tourist attraction.

Mr. L'Amour now lives in Los Angeles with his wife Kathy, who helps with the enormous amount of research he does for his books. Soon, Mr. L'Amour hopes, the children (Beau and Angelique) will be helping too.

BANTAM'S #1
ALL-TIME BESTSELLING AUTHOR
AMERICA'S FAVORITE WESTERN WRITER

☐	13561	THE STRONG SHALL LIVE	$1.95
☐	12354	BENDIGO SHAFTER	$2.25
☐	13881	THE KEY-LOCK MAN	$1.95
☐	13719	RADIGAN	$1.95
☐	13609	WAR PARTY	$1.95
☐	13882	KIOWA TRAIL	$1.95
☐	13683	THE BURNING HILLS	$1.95
☐	12064	SHALAKO	$1.75
☐	13680	KILRONE	$1.95
☐	13794	THE RIDER OF LOST CREEK	$1.95
☐	13798	CALLAGHEN	$1.95
☐	14114	THE QUICK AND THE DEAD	$1.95
☐	14219	OVER ON THE DRY SIDE	$1.95
☐	13722	DOWN THE LONG HILLS	$1.95
☐	14316	WESTWARD THE TIDE	$1.95
☐	12043	KID RODELO	$1.75
☐	14104	BROKEN GUN	$1.95
☐	13898	WHERE THE LONG GRASS BLOWS	$1.95
☐	12519	HOW THE WEST WAS WON	$1.75

**Buy them at your local bookstore or use this
handy coupon for ordering:**

Bantam Books, Inc., Dept. LL2, 414 East Golf Road, Des Plaines, Ill. 60016

Please send me the books I have checked above. I am enclosing $_____
(please add $1.00 to cover postage and handling). Send check or money order
—no cash or C.O.D.'s please.

Mr/Mrs/Miss _____

Address _____

City _____ State/Zip _____

LL2—8/80

Please allow four to six weeks for delivery. This offer expires 12/80.

BANTAM'S #1
ALL-TIME BESTSELLING AUTHOR
AMERICA'S FAVORITE WESTERN WRITER

☐	13601	HIGH LONESOME	$1.95
☐	13704	BORDEN CHANTRY	$1.95
☐	13606	BRIONNE	$1.95
☐	13501	THE FERGUSON RIFLE	$1.75
☐	13622	KILLOE	$1.95
☐	13602	CONAGHER	$1.95
☐	14121	NORTH TO THE RAILS	$1.95
☐	13879	THE MAN FROM SKIBBEREEN	$1.95
☐	14159	SILVER CANYON	$1.95
☐	13857	CATLOW	$1.95
☐	13611	GUNS OF THE TIMBERLANDS	$1.95
☐	13605	HANGING WOMAN CREEK	$1.95
☐	13717	FALLON	$1.95
☐	13779	UNDER THE SWEETWATER RIM	$1.95
☐	13152	MATAGORDA	$1.75
☐	14119	DARK CANYON	$1.95
☐	13684	THE CALIFORNIOS	$1.95
☐	13969	FLINT	$1.95

Buy them at your local bookstore or use this
handy coupon for ordering:

Bantam Books, Inc., Dept. LL1, 414 East Golf Road, Des Plaines, Ill. 60016

Please send me the books I have checked above. I am enclosing $_____
(please add $1.00 to cover postage and handling). Send check or money order
—no cash or C.O.D.'s please.

Mr/Mrs/Miss_____

Address_____

City_____State/Zip_____

LL1—5/80

Please allow four to six weeks for delivery. This offer expires 11/80.

Bantam Book Catalog

Here's your up-to-the-minute listing of over 1,400 titles by your favorite authors.

This illustrated, large format catalog gives a description of each title. For your convenience, it is divided into categories in fiction and non-fiction—gothics, science fiction, westerns, mysteries, cookbooks, mysticism and occult, biographies, history, family living, health, psychology, art.

So don't delay—take advantage of this special opportunity to increase your reading pleasure.

Just send us your name and address and 50¢ (to help defray postage and handling costs).